AVENGERS AND ROGUES

THE J.R. FINN SAILING MYSTERY SERIES

C.L.R. DOUGHERTY

AVENGERS AND ROGUES

The J.R. Finn Sailing Mystery Series
Book 2

Corruption and Revenge in the Caribbean and Florida

1

I WAS STANDING NECK-DEEP IN THE WARM WATER OFF THE ROCKY beach below the target's villa. The wind was out of the north-east, so the land mass of St. Thomas blocked the sloppy seas that were running in open water.

I anchored my dinghy among the reefs off Deck Point, a few hundred yards from where I stood. The spot where I left it was well-protected, and the adjacent shoreline was overgrown. The dinghy was well-hidden. I waded along the point until I turned the corner into Jersey Bay, making my swim to the villa's private beach shorter than I expected.

The calm water was a mixed blessing. Swimming was easy, but I couldn't afford to splash. Any disturbance in the water's glassy surface would reflect the ambient light from the houses ashore, announcing my presence to anyone who was watching. An accidental splash would give me away to the target's security people.

A steep set of stairs led up from the little beach. From where I stood, I couldn't see the access from the stairs to the compound. I was too close; the perspective was wrong.

Using a slow breaststroke to avoid roiling the water's

surface, I swam out into the bay a hundred yards and turned around, treading water. That solved my perspective problem, but I was too far away to make out details in the dim light. The properties on either side of the target's compound were better lighted than the target's.

The absence of lighting on the stairs to the target's place might have been a vulnerability for him, or maybe his security measures included motion sensors of some sort. The only way to find out was for me to go ashore. In a black wetsuit with my face covered in camouflage paint, I would be all right, but I dared not use the stairs. I breaststroked my way back to the beach.

In neck-deep water again, I studied the approach from the beach to the stairs. Working my way in closer to shore, I discovered that the beach was quite steep. As I got into the shallows, I lowered myself to a prone position. Moving slowly to avoid detection, I used a cheap cellphone to scan for infrared light sources.

Unlike more expensive digital cameras, the phone's camera lacked an infrared filter. If someone caught me with it or searched my boat and found it, the phone wouldn't arouse suspicion the way a more sophisticated infrared detector might. It would make me look like a cheapskate instead of a spy. My low-tech IR detector wasn't as sensitive or as precise as the good ones. That was its downside.

I crawled to the right end of the beach and aimed the phone across to the left end, swinging it back and forth as I watched the screen. Spotting nothing, I slithered through the water to the other end of the beach and repeated the process.

Satisfied that there weren't any IR beams to set off an alarm, I crawled up onto the beach. The surface was hard-packed sand with a few pebbles. My weight might have caused crunching sounds, so I moved slowly. For all I knew there were listening devices.

I made it to the foot of the stairs in a low crawl, holding my belly just off the ground. I dared not use the stairs themselves. There could have been pressure sensors or night vision cameras protecting that approach. Instead, I picked my way through the scrub, crawling parallel to the right side of the wooden staircase, my belly an inch from the ground.

It took me a couple of minutes to draw level with the top of the stairs. The staircase ended at a 12-foot-square deck with a fence on the opposite side. The fence was wrought iron, about eight feet high, and it bordered on a swimming pool area in front of the villa.

The fence's gate was closed, probably locked, but there wasn't enough light for me to tell for sure. The fence ran about 50 yards each way from the gate. It joined a concrete wall that enclosed the compound. The wall was a couple of feet higher than the fence.

With my chin level with the surface of the deck, I got a clear view of the villa on the other side of the pool. It was of modern design; the wall facing the pool was made entirely of glass. The inside lighting was subdued; it was three o'clock in the morning. Everyone inside was probably asleep. There wasn't enough light for me to learn much more about the interior.

There was a scrabbling sound from somewhere between me and the gate. A fraction of a second later, I was blinded by floodlights illuminating the area in front of me. Resisting the urge to move out of the way, I watched as two men burst from a cabana at the left end of the pool.

Both armed with AK-47s, they rushed to opposite ends of the wrought iron fence and crouched, their eyes scanning the area outside the fence. They swept the muzzles of their weapons back and forth as they stared in my direction.

Grateful for the cover provided by clumps of monkey grass, I froze. I closed my eyes lest their reflection give me away.

"Damned iguanas again," one of the men said, rising to his feet and lowering the muzzle of his assault rifle.

"Ought to waste the scaly little shits," the other one said. "Every damn night, they do this."

They ambled back to the cabana and ducked inside as the lights shut off.

I was grateful to the iguanas. Now I knew a little more about the target's security. At least two men on watch, armed. Lights with some sort of motion sensors. I couldn't cross the open area between the top of the stairs and the gate.

They blamed iguanas, but the guards were alert and quick to respond. The route I took up the side of the staircase was clear of sensors; otherwise, the guards would have challenged me.

My goal that night was reconnaissance; I was scoping the place out before I decided how to engage. Getting up to deck level again wouldn't be a problem, but I needed to find a way into the compound. To avoid the gate and the wrought iron fence, I would have to go over the concrete wall.

I backed down the rocky face of the bluff. With my head below the edge, I crabbed my way to the right, since I was already on the right side of the stairs. As I got farther from the stairs, the face of the bluff became closer to vertical. Using clumps of scrub and the occasional rocky outcropping for hand and footholds, I traversed what I estimated to be 50 yards.

Thinking I should be directly below the corner where the wrought iron fence met the concrete wall, I climbed back up a couple of feet and peered over the edge. I was where I wanted to be. Taking out my phone, I scanned for infrared light beams again. When I didn't find any, I eased my way up and over the edge of the bluff.

Belly to the ground, I worked my way through the low scrub until I reached the corner of the fence. Between the wall and the adjacent property, there was an overgrown, vacant lot that was a couple of hundred yards wide.

Rising to my hands and knees, I followed the wall back toward Deck Point Road, away from the beach. Fifty yards in from the corner, the scrub on the vacant lot was high enough so that I could stand without risk of being silhouetted.

My earlier estimate of the wall's height was correct; it was ten feet. Without something to stand on, I wouldn't be able to reach the top edge. With a running start, I could vault high enough to get a handhold and pull myself up.

That was risky, though, since I didn't know what was on the top of the wall. There could have been broken glass embedded in the concrete, or motion detectors. I pushed my way into the undergrowth until I was a few feet from the wall. Finding a dead palm tree that was still standing, I shimmied up it a few feet.

Looking toward the target's house, I could see over the top of the wall. There was enough light for me to pick out the glint of broken glass along its top. With my left arm wrapped around the tree trunk, I pulled my makeshift IR detector out of the waterproof zippered pouch at my waist.

Sweeping the phone back and forth, I picked up an IR light source on top of the wall in the direction of the road. The beam no doubt ran along the top of the wall to a receiver at the corner where the wrought iron fence joined the concrete.

The wall looked to be a foot thick, and the beam was roughly a foot above its top. That was too low to sneak under and too high to get over without a little help. That was okay; I could deal with that, since I knew it was there.

Shifting my attention to what was on the other side of the wall, I saw that there was an open area between the fence and the side of the villa. The villa didn't have any windows that faced the fence.

I wasn't up high enough to see the ground inside the

compound, but up under the villa's eaves I saw a cluster of floodlights on each corner. The lights were aimed down at the patch of ground between the villa and the wall. Given that there were no windows in that end of the villa, there must be cameras. The flood lights were there for security. They were probably triggered by motion detectors, like the ones I saw earlier.

Where were the iguanas when I needed them? I shimmied down the tree trunk and shuffled around in the darkness until I found a coconut. Picking it up, I took several quick steps toward the wall and heaved it over.

As I heard the soft thump of the coconut landing, the flood lights flared. In a few seconds, I heard the guards.

"Another friggin' false alarm. Damn iguanas."

"Yeah. Well, shit. It's what he's payin' us for," a second voice said.

"He's not even here, man. Why we gotta do this?"

"Because it's what he's payin' us for. One time it might not be the iguanas."

"When's he coming back?"

"I dunno, man. Not our worry. They took a lot of shit with 'em to Miami, though. Looked like they was gonna stay for a while. Come on; let's finish watchin' the movie."

The target was out of town. When would he be back? Where was he? My client would be able to help with that. It was time for me to go back to the boat.

2

I WAS CRAWLING THROUGH THE UNDERBRUSH ALONG THE EAST side of the staircase making my way back to the beach when I heard them. Their voices marked them as the same two men who were griping about the iguanas.

They were speaking softly, but the sound carried, and I was on high alert. I froze, sinking to the ground, melting into the vegetation. The treads of the stairs creaking under their weight told me they weren't moving fast. As they came abreast of my position, I was able to make out what they were saying.

"He's full of shit; he just wants to order us around while the boss ain't here. It's nothin' but the damn iguanas."

"Uh-uh. He said the IR cameras picked up a guy in the woods east of the wall. Said he threw something over; that's what tripped the floodlights in the side yard."

"Then why the hell send us to the beach?"

"Because of the lights on the stair landing. Remember?"

"Yeah, but there wasn't nobody there; we woulda seen 'em. He shoulda sent us to check out the woods."

"He sent Harris and Jackson to watch the road. Figures if we're watchin' the beach, we got the guy boxed in. He goes out to the road, Harris and Jackson'll get him. He comes back to the beach, it's you and me."

"We s'posed to waste him?"

"Nope. Capture him and take him inside. He wants to interrogate him."

"Might be fun..."

I rolled onto my back and threw a fist-sized rock in a high arc over the stairway. It crashed into the brush several yards downhill from their position.

They clammed up and dropped to their knees, weapons pointed toward the noise. I heard one of them whisper a few words. Then a flashlight beam cut through the darkness, sweeping the undergrowth on the opposite side of the stairs from me.

"We know you're out there," one of them said. "Stand up with your hands in the air. You got 'til the count of three, then it's too late. One... two... three."

"Now what?" the other one whispered.

I heard one of them working the action on his AK-47, chambering a round.

"No, dumbass!" the second one said.

The flashlight beam swung up to the sky. The one with the light used it to push the other one's rifle up, barrel pointing at the stars.

"Well, I warned — "

"You can't shoot up the damn hillside, you moron."

"But — "

"It was probably one of them damned iguanas. Friggin' overgrown lizards. Put the safety on and let's get down to the beach."

The moron grumbled something I couldn't hear, and they shut off the light. After a few seconds of whispered conversation, the stairs began to creak again. I lay motionless, giving them time to get down to the beach.

Once I heard their footsteps crunching in the gravel and sand, I started moving. If I inadvertently made a noise, their attention would be drawn to the area where I tossed the rock.

That's just the way people are wired. I was holding another rock in my fist, in case I needed to reinforce their misunderstanding of the situation. As I crept along, I pondered the new information.

There were at least three other security people. Jackson, Harris, and whoever was in charge. If they were all as inept as those two, I was in good shape.

Crawling down the bluff toward the beach, I considered my options. Even as careless as these two were, I wouldn't have been able to cross the beach from the undergrowth without being seen. The crunching of the gravel would have given me away.

I was in a hurry; the sun would be up soon. There was no good place for me to hide in daylight, so my choices were limited. I needed to put those two out of commission.

Their assault rifles made me nervous. I wasn't worried about getting shot; I was confident I could disarm them without that happening. One of the two was trigger-happy, though. If he opened fire, the noise would be a problem; it would alert the other security people.

I needed to disable those two for long enough to allow me to swim away. I didn't want their friends standing on the beach shooting at me while I was in the water.

I was approaching the edge of the scrub. My two adversaries were standing on the beach, looking up the stairs. They figured that's where I would come from.

They weren't over 20 feet from me, and they were standing almost shoulder to shoulder. That was good; I could use the one closer to me as cover when I rushed them.

I carried a blackjack in the pouch at my waist. Unzipping

the pouch, careful not to make a sound, I gripped the weighted end of the blackjack in my left hand.

Pulling my legs up under myself, I dug my toes into the sand as I rose slightly, taking my weight on my left arm. I was in a crouch, ready to lurch forward.

I rolled to my left and threw my second rock as far as I could toward the other side of the stairs. When it hit the brush, the two guards turned toward the sound. I charged them.

The one closer to me was sweeping the area where the rock landed with the flashlight. The other one was tracking the beam of the flashlight with his weapon.

Neither noticed the crunch of my footfalls. I sprinted a few steps as I shifted the blackjack to my right hand, and then I was on top of the closer man. He sensed my presence and started to turn toward me as I smacked him on the temple with the blackjack.

Grabbing him as he collapsed, I used my momentum to shove him into the second man. While he was trying to untangle himself from his unconscious sidekick, I hit him as well. I delivered a second blow to each, just to be sure they were unconscious.

Picking up the flashlight, I turned it off and wiped it down to make sure I didn't leave fingerprints. Satisfied they wouldn't wake up soon, I turned and waded out until the water was deep enough for me to swim.

3

AFTER SWIMMING BACK TO THE DINGHY, I MOTORED ACROSS THE channel to my boat, *Carib Princess,* in the Christmas Cove anchorage at Great Saint James Island. I went below and got a beer, taking it up to the cockpit to help me unwind from my adventure.

Four days ago, I left Rodney Bay, St. Lucia. Yesterday I made my landfall in the U.S. Virgin Islands at St. John, where I cleared myself into the U.S. with customs and immigration. My paperwork was clean, which was important.

Before Rodney Bay, I was in Ste. Anne, Martinique. I was half of a happy cruising couple when I got there, but things changed fast, sometimes. The lady who was with me got into a little difficulty that left several people dead on a megayacht. She departed from Martinique without stopping to tell me goodbye.

Fortunately, she left her passport aboard *Carib Princess.* With that and a gratuity to a travel agent, I was able to get her name off my ship's papers and secure my outbound clearance from Martinique. I left a couple of hours after I discovered what she did. The next morning, I made a clean entrance into

Rodney Bay with St. Lucia's customs and immigration people when their office opened.

The sail from Ste. Anne to Rodney Bay only takes a few hours; it's about 20 miles. It took me a little longer because I disposed of two bodies *en route*. While my lady was wreaking havoc on those people aboard that megayacht, two of their friends came looking for me on *Carib Princess*. The lady was just a friend, but those fools thought I was working with her. That mistake cost them their lives.

Before I returned to my boat from clearing in, I received an encrypted text from my client. That was what I called them since I retired. They used to be my employer, and I still did contract work for them from time to time. I wasn't allowed to say who they were, but my retirement checks came from the U.S. Army.

I spent a few years in the Army before my client discovered my true talent. They kept me on the Army's rolls, but my chain of command changed. I worked for a small department of the government that made use of my particular skills.

That was why I was in St. Thomas — to use my skills to solve a problem for my client. The problem was embodied in a native-born U.S. citizen of Syrian descent named Daoud Nasser, and he was staying in the villa I just visited.

Daoud Nasser was his birth name, but he changed it legally to David Nash somewhere along the way. Nash was a known member of ISIS. He was working with ISIS in Syria. That made him a wanted man in the States. Nash starred in a cellphone video on a phone confiscated from a dead ISIS fighter in Syria two years ago. I didn't know what the video showed, but whatever it was, it was worth Nash's life.

Nobody knew what Nash was doing from the time the video was made until he came to St. Thomas. Facial recognition software picked him up at immigration when he flew in from Paris a month ago. He set up housekeeping in that rented villa I scouted earlier. The rental was in his new name, David Nash, and he signed a year's lease.

The client tracked him until the warrant for his execution came through. Recently, Nash took one of the high-speed ferries to Tortola twice to meet an unidentified man. With the warrant in hand, my client suggested that I could nail Nash in Tortola, since it was British territory.

I chuckled at the client's naïveté. Typical of desk jockeys, my client was aghast at the idea of killing a U.S. citizen on U.S. soil. They suggested that I watch for him at the ferry terminal in Red Hook and follow him to the BVI, but that was no good. I was much less likely to get in trouble for killing him in St. Thomas. It was like the Wild West compared to the BVI. But it didn't matter where I killed him. I never got in trouble.

To get in trouble, I had to get caught. My unusual talent was that I never got caught. Careful reconnaissance was the key to a successful assassination, and that was why I was anchored here in Christmas Cove.

The target's compound was less than a mile away on the southeast corner of St. Thomas. I couldn't quite see his villa from my anchorage; it was hidden behind Deck Point, the spit of land that separated Cowpet Cove from Jersey Bay. I timed my trip earlier, though. From here, I could reach Nash's private beach in ten minutes.

It was possible to scramble over the rocks from Deck Point, where I landed the dinghy, and approach the villa from Deck Point Road. Given that I might have extra time before Nash came back, I could scout that route tomorrow night. It never hurt to have a backup plan.

Approaching from the beach was less likely to attract attention. Nash was not an amateur. He and his security people would see the land side as more vulnerable.

There was also the question of how to eliminate the target. If I killed him in U.S. territory, an accident would be best, but it wasn't the only way. I needed to know more about his behavior before I worried too much about how to carry out my mission. That meant more reconnaissance.

A drug-related killing could be as believable as an accident, depending on his activities. St. Thomas was a hotbed of drug trafficking. Mid-level drug smugglers were forever killing one another in this part of the world. It could be as simple as planting contraband or cash among the bodies. His security people would have to be part of the package if I chose that option.

An accident might have allowed me to spare Nash's troops, which would have pleased my client. But operational details were my call, and a credible accident was harder to arrange than an outright killing. I figured whoever was guarding this piece of garbage was no better than he was. The more the merrier as far as making it look like the work of a cartel.

But Nash wasn't in residence, so I needed to check with the client for an update on his whereabouts.

4

I WOKE UP IN THE COCKPIT, STILL IN MY WETSUIT. THE SUNRISE roused me. Glancing at my watch, I saw I'd slept for less than an hour. I went below and loaded my coffee pot, firing up the stove. While the coffee perked, I took a quick shower to rinse off the salt and sand.

Refreshed and wearing dry shorts and a T-shirt, I sat down at the table in the main cabin with my satellite phone and a cup of coffee. It was too early to call the client, so I composed a text message instead.

I didn't give them details of last night's surveillance; that would have made them nervous. I wanted them to know that David Nash was away from the compound on St. Thomas for an indeterminate amount of time. The security guards seemed to think he wasn't coming back any time soon.

If the guard was right about Nash going to Miami, my client would need to sound the alarm with the Department of Homeland Security. Or maybe they would order me to Miami. That would be unusual, but Nash was an unusual target.

The scary thing about his being in St. Thomas was that he could go anywhere in the U.S. without passing through immigration or any other security checkpoints. He was raised as an American; the bastard was born in the States. He knew his way around our country.

Not only did he have freedom of movement, but he was a wealthy man. Nash could do a great deal of damage unless somebody stopped him. And there was every reason to assume that he wasn't in the U.S. because he got homesick for baseball games and hot dogs.

With the text on its way, I was having second thoughts about that coffee. I needed more sleep, not caffeine. Stepping into the galley, I took a vacuum bottle out of the locker beside the stove and decanted the coffee into it.

It was 6 o'clock in the morning in the Virgin Islands. I wasn't likely to hear anything from the client for a few hours. I could catch up on my sleep. I put the thermos of coffee and the encrypted satellite phone on the saloon table and stretched out on the settee for a nap.

———

THE RINGING of the satellite phone woke me from a sound sleep. I wasn't fast enough to get to it before the caller hung up, but only my client could call that phone. A quick look at the clock told me I slept for three hours. Allowing for the time difference, it was 8 o'clock in Virginia, where my client's office was located.

I poured a mug of coffee from the thermos and picked up the phone. It looked like a regular, commercially available satellite phone, but it wasn't. After I keyed in the access code, the screen told me I missed a call from an unknown number.

That was the client. As I said, this wasn't a normal phone. It only accepted calls from one number — the client's. I used the cursor keys to highlight the little voicemail icon and pressed the enter key. After I entered another, different passcode, I heard the recorded message.

"Urgent that you return this call. We need to discuss your recent text regarding the missing shipment. We're waiting."

It was the woman who assigned my targets for most of my career. Her voice was as familiar as my own.

I went through the convoluted routine to return the call from "unknown caller." After one ring, I heard a series of clicks and tones as the call was routed through a random series of relays. The woman answered.

"Extension 4235. State your callback ID, please."

"Callback ID is 691414," I said.

"You recognize my voice?" she asked.

"Yes."

"And you've been authenticated," she said. "Are you alone?"

"Yes."

"When did you discover the shipment was missing?"

"Three a.m., local time."

"In St. Thomas?"

"Yes."

"And how confident are you that it was mis-routed to Miami?"

"Not very, but that's what I overheard."

"And was there damage to any of the goods in storage at your end?"

"Minor," I said. "Nothing that will take more than a couple of hours to repair."

"Good. I don't suppose you have an address in Miami for the shipment?"

"No."

"How about the means of shipment?"

"No, sorry," I said. "I didn't hear anything about that."

"Is that young woman still sailing with you?"

"No."

"Where is she?" she asked.

"I have no idea. Why?"

"I'm asking the questions. Did you give her that passport we arranged?"

"Yes, but — "

She cut me off. "Just answer my questions."

I didn't say anything.

"Hello? Are you there?"

"Yes."

"Why didn't you respond to my statement?" she asked.

"It was a statement."

"So what?"

"So you said to just answer your questions."

"Still the same old smart-ass."

"I'm getting bored with this conversation."

"Tough," she said.

"I'm retired, remember?"

"Why is that relevant?"

"I don't have to do this. That's why."

"What are you getting at?"

"You can't just waltz in and screw with me anymore. You need to buy me candy, send flowers, maybe. Suck up to me, if you want me to do your bidding."

"What do you want?" she asked.

"Why did you ask about the girl?"

"We haven't seen any recent activity on the passport we got for her."

"No, you haven't. She doesn't have it any longer."

"You said you gave it to her."

"I did. But when we parted ways, she left it with me."

"So you still have it?"

"Yes. Why?"

"Some of our relatives are looking for her. Do you know if she has a different passport?"

"I'd be surprised if she didn't."

"Do you know what name she's using?"

"No."

"Do you know anything about her?" she asked.

"A little."

"What's your relationship with her?"

"Purely personal. I'm getting annoyed with this."

"We got you a passport for her, no questions."

"And I appreciate it, but you've used up the goodwill from that. Why the questions about her?"

"She's wanted for questioning about several murders of organized crime figures. Our relatives were about to arrest them, but they think she blew them away. Does that surprise you?"

"No."

"Did you know about that?"

"Yes."

"Were you part of it?"

"No. But they were asking for it. She gave them what they deserved."

"If you say so. We hear two of her possible victims are still missing, unaccounted for. Know anything about that?"

"Maybe. You got names?"

"Only one matters. His name's Frankie Dailey. He's supposedly a confidential informant for our relatives. Heard of him?"

"Yeah, but not lately. And our relatives shouldn't expect to, either. He got some bad fish."

"Bad fish? I don't..."

"They ate him, the bad fish did."

"Do you have personal knowledge of that?"

"Yes. It was self-defense. He started it. The fish were just doing what fish do."

"I see. Will you see the girl again?"

"I hope so. You got a problem with that?"

"No. As long as she's not mixed up in our business."

"Okay. I get that. Now what about the missing shipment?"

"We're working on that. You still interested in helping us out?"

"Sure. You want me to ask around at the origin address? See if they know anything?"

"Not just yet. But can you do that if we need for you to?"

"Yeah. It may damage more goods, but I can handle it on the quiet. It won't come back on us."

"Hold off. We just started tracking the shipment. I'll give it a few hours. You stand by where you are until you hear from me."

"Okay. No problem. Anything else?"

"Yeah. About the girl."

"What about her?"

"We're good with that, just between you and me. You're entitled to a little companionship. Just be careful. I don't want to lose you in a mob crossfire after all we've been through."

"Thanks."

"Don't mention it. I'll get back to you on the shipment."

She hung up, and I finally took a sip of the coffee I poured before I returned her call. It was stone cold. That was the longest I ever talked with her since I started taking orders from her years ago.

And it was the first time we ever discussed anything that bordered on personal. I always wondered about her, wondered what she was like. But we had never met, and we never would. That was the way this worked, the way we stayed under cover.

5

WITH TIME ON MY HANDS AS I FINISHED THE THERMOS OF COFFEE, my thoughts turned to Mary. That was the girl my client mentioned, or at least that was the name she was using when we met.

Mary and I were in the same line of work, but for different people. As best I knew, she was a freelance operator. Mary and I never got a chance to discuss the details of her working arrangements.

We met by accident in a little fishing village called Puerto Real, on Puerto Rico's west coast. At least, I thought it was by accident. I wasn't sure about that. The story she told me then was that she was on the run from some bad people.

I believed that at the time, because three of them tried to kidnap her within a few minutes after we met. I helped her avoid their clutches, and we sailed together for a few weeks, but that was another story.

They caught up with her about a week ago when we were relaxing in Ste. Anne, Martinique. Or maybe she caught up with them; it was hard to tell.

Anyway, as my client suggested, Mary got the better of

them. She left in a hurry with a trail of bodies behind her. She killed them all, except the two who came looking for me.

Frankie Dailey, the one who was "supposedly" a confidential informant for "our relatives" — that would be the FBI — was the one who told me Mary was a killer for hire. He and one of his minions tried to capture me and take me to Frankie's yacht.

He meant to question me along with Mary, but it didn't work out the way he planned. If he was working for the FBI, I was Mother Teresa's long-lost son.

After he told me everything he knew about Mary, he and his sidekick passed away right here aboard *Carib Princess*. Then I went to Frankie's yacht to see if Mary needed help, but she was already on her way out of town when I got there.

I got a text from her later; she wanted to meet me in Puerto Real in a few weeks to resume our friendship. That gave me an incentive to wrap up this David Nash business in a hurry.

I was glad my client had no objection to my relationship with Mary. But I wasn't about to share my plans for meeting her. The client didn't have a need to know, as they say in the spook business.

It was thanks to Mary's problems that I changed the name of my boat to *Carib Princess*. Now that I was back in U.S. waters, I planned to restore her original name. That way, my own identity would be slightly more obscure, just in case anything untoward happened.

Taking out my tools, I cut into the fiberglass that covered the lead ballast in the boat's keel. A strongbox rested atop the cast-lead plug.

I opened the strongbox and put Mary's old passport — the one my client asked about — in a file folder with several others. The passport Mary used when I met her was in there already; the rest were mine, in several names.

Being able to change identities at will was important to my

health. From another folder, I took out one of several U.S. Coast Guard Certificates of Documentation for this boat. It showed the vessel name as *Island Girl*. That was my favorite. I put the document for *Carib Princess* in the folder.

Next, I picked up a piece of loosely rolled waxed paper. It was the backing for a set of vinyl transfer letters spelling out *Island Girl*. I put that on the chart table along with the new Coast Guard certificate and closed the strong box.

A half hour later, I finished laying up new fiberglass to conceal the strong box. I would have to paint the glass work to finish the job, but the epoxy resin needed a day to cure before I could paint over it.

Up on deck, I launched the inflatable dinghy and tied it off alongside. I retrieved the vinyl transfer lettering and a bag containing acetone, rags, and a package of single-edge razor blades.

Climbing down into the dinghy, I untied it and moved it around to the stern. It took me five minutes to scrape off the *Carib Princess* name. I cleaned the surface of the transom with acetone and the rags.

While it dried, I unrolled the new lettering. Using a fingernail, I picked at a corner of the backing paper that covered the adhesive on the lettering. Once I got it started, I positioned the unrolled sheet of lettering on the transom and secured it with tape across the top.

Reaching underneath, I gripped the free corner and pulled it. Peeling off the backing, I used my other hand to smooth the vinyl letters in place. In a few minutes, I untaped the transfer sheet and smoothed the last few bubbles out of the letters.

My boat was once again *Island Girl*. I'm not sure why that was important to me, but it was part of my identity. Living the way I did, there weren't many fixed reference points in my life. *Island Girl* was one of them.

Moving the dinghy back alongside, I set my bag of stuff on

the side deck and climbed up. After I hoisted the dinghy and put my supplies away, I opened a beer and stretched out in the cockpit under the awning.

I was feeling retired again, at least until I got another message from my client. With any luck, that might not be until tomorrow.

6

THE SQUAWK OF A LOUD-HAILER WOKE ME FROM MY NAP. I looked in the sound's direction and saw an orange U.S. Coast Guard launch — an RB-S, or Response Boat -Small — in their jargon. There were two uniformed men in the pilothouse and two more standing at the side closest to *Island Girl*, ready to come alongside. There was also a fit-looking civilian in a dark suit, sweat running down his face.

"Good morning, captain," one of the uniformed crewmen said. "Is anyone else aboard?"

"No, I'm by myself. What's up?"

"Courtesy boarding," he said. "Do you have any weapons aboard?"

"No."

He turned and nodded to the man at the helm. I heard the clunk of the two big outboards shifting into forward. Water boiled behind the launch, and they came alongside. The uniformed men vaulted *Island Girl's* lifelines and turned to help the guy in the suit. He was agile enough, but he didn't have the practiced ease of the coastguardsmen. He got aboard, though, with their help. The RB-S pulled back a few feet, drifting.

"Special Agent George Kelley, FBI," the suit said, approaching me with his hand extended. As I shook hands with him, he said, "You're Jerome Finnegan, correct?"

I nodded, hiding my surprise. *This is no routine "courtesy boarding."*

"Come up front with me, Mr. Finnegan. We can talk while they handle the search." Kelley turned and went to the foredeck, ducking awkwardly to get past the rigging.

Search? Odd choice of words for someone involved in a routine boarding, but what the hell. The Coast Guard doesn't need a warrant, not for a U.S. flagged vessel in U.S. waters. But this dumbass just tipped his hand and confirmed that this wasn't a routine boarding. So what does he want?

I followed him up to the foredeck and sat down on the forward end of the coachroof.

"What brings you to St. Thomas, Mr. Finnegan?"

"Finn will do just fine, Mr. Kelley."

"It's Special Agent Kelley. And I asked you a question."

So you're not just a garden variety dumbass. You're an asshole, to boot. Okay. We can do it that way.

I plastered a shit-eating grin on my face and said, "The wind."

"What? The wind? What about the wind?"

"Just answering your question."

"Huh?"

"Get with the program, Kelley. You — "

"It's Special Agent Kelley."

"Right. You asked what brought me to St. Thomas. This is a sailboat. The wind brought me to St. Thomas."

"Okay, smart-ass. We can do this downtown, at the federal building."

"Gonna arrest me, Kelley?" I watched the flush spread up from his collar. "Be careful how you answer that. It might be a trick question."

"What the hell's the matter with you? I'm an FBI agent. Mess around with me and I'll tie your ass up in red tape for days, even if you're innocent. And everybody's guilty of something."

"Really? I've got lots of time. And money for lawyers. Why don't you knock off the bullshit and tell me why you're here?"

"It's a routine Coast Guard boarding."

"No, Special Agent Kelley. It's not. FBI agents aren't part of a routine boarding. And you knew my name before you set foot aboard. So you gave yourself away. Sorry to react this way, but I feel like you're screwing around with me. Why don't we start over and you tell me why you're here? Maybe we can work something out."

"I could still take you downtown," Kelley said.

"Yep. I'd go with you. But if you do that, I'll have to make a phone call to some people in Washington. That's a rule I have to follow because of my old line of work. I can't tell you about that part, but trust me. If that happens, shit's gonna rain down on both of us. It would be a lot better if you told me what you need. Cut the bullshit, and I'll help you if I can."

"Are you threatening me, Finn?"

"Nope. I'm offering to help you. You were the one making threats. All I'm doing is trying to put our conversation back on the rails. I'm sorry I ruffled your feathers, but the easiest way out of this for both of us is for you to just shoot straight with me. We've both been around the block a few times, I'm sure."

He scowled at me for several seconds. "Your paperwork says you're retired. But were you some kind of cop? A spook or something?"

"I really can't answer questions about that, okay? I was telling you the truth about that phone call I'd have to make. It would be better if you and I could work this out right here, between us. Sorry we got off on the wrong foot."

"Okay, but don't push your luck, Finn. I have some questions. You give me straight answers, and we'll forget all this happened. Unless the boys find something they shouldn't. I can't do much about that."

"Fair enough. Tell me what you need."

"You had a woman aboard for a few weeks. Mary Elizabeth O'Brien. We think she hitched a ride with you from Puerto Rico to Bequia. That right?"

"Yes, that's right." *As far as it goes.* "Can you tell me what this is about?"

He chewed on his lip for a few seconds.

"It's a long story, but it starts with a double murder in Florida," Kelley said. "A developer and his wife who were laundering drug money. Guy named Dailey. Mean anything to you?"

"I read about it in the papers, but the story fizzled out. Did they catch whoever did it?"

"That's why I'm here."

"I don't know anything about the Daileys. Or drug money."

"No. But we think the O'Brien woman might know something. That's why we're trying to track her down."

"I see. Like you said, she hitched a ride with me. She said she was between jobs, looking for a paid crew position on a big yacht."

"Why would she have gone to Bequia?" Kelley asked. "Seems to me there would be better places to find crew jobs."

"Yeah, you're right. She said she was burned out on Puerto Rico, wanted to find something on a European yacht, maybe. She told me she'd had a job on a big yacht out of Miami that got her to Puerto Rico, but it didn't work out." *I expected him to pick up on that. Ask me questions about it. At least the name of the yacht.*

"But why Bequia?"

"Sorry. I got sidetracked. I was headed for the Eastern Caribbean. You sail?"

"No. Why?"

"I didn't want to tell you stuff you'd already know. To get to the east on a sailboat down here, it's easier if you take a less direct route. Her best bet for crew jobs on European yachts would have been maybe St. Martin, or Antigua, or one of the French islands. But that would have meant pounding straight into the trade winds from Puerto Rico. So we took off at an angle to the wind. Picked one that gave us the best boat speed. And that took us to Bequia. To go north from there to the other islands, it's an easy sail with the wind on the beam, see."

"Okay. So you're saying Bequia wasn't really a destination? Just a stop along the way?"

"Exactly."

"And you just happened to be going where she wanted to go? That it? Or were you going to Bequia anyway?"

"I'm retired, remember? I just sail for the fun of it. One island's as good as another, for me."

"Must be nice to live like that."

"I'm not complaining. It beats working, for sure."

"And then the two of you sailed north to Ste. Anne, Martinique, from Bequia. That correct?"

Now, how did you know that? Mary and I went to great lengths to change our names and the boat's name so we couldn't be tracked through any of the customs and immigration databases. That's why Island Girl was named Carib Princess when I got here. For that matter, how the hell did you find me this morning? It's only been two hours since I changed her name back to Island Girl.

"Yeah, that's right. Martinique."

"How long were you in Martinique?"

"Two days, give or take. Living like this, it's tough to keep track. You want me to check my logbook?"

"Not just yet. That's okay. And from there, you went to St. Lucia? Rodney Bay?"

"Yes."

How the hell does he know? Was somebody following me?

"She was still with you? In Rodney Bay?"

"No. She found something in Martinique, I guess. I got a text from her saying goodbye. That's when I left."

"So she didn't come here with you, then?"

"That's right. I sailed here solo from St. Lucia."

"Why'd you go to St. Lucia first?"

"That wind thing, again. To get a better angle on the wind. Sailing downwind's not as tricky as sailing into the wind, but some angles to the wind are better than others, even downwind."

"I see. And you came here because..."

"Homesick for the good old U.S. of A. Anything else I can tell you?"

"No, not for now. You gonna be here for a while?"

I shrugged. "I just got here. Still recovering from the trip. But there's nothing to keep me here. The good part of being retired is I have no plans. And I stick to them religiously."

He frowned at that.

"That's a joke," I said.

He nodded. "Looks like they finished checking over the boat."

I looked over my shoulder and saw the two coastguardsmen sitting in the cockpit, one with a clipboard in his hand.

"Should we join them?" I asked. "They're probably looking for my signature."

"Yeah."

Kelley took a business card from the side pocket of his suit coat and handed it to me. "Call me if you think of anything that might help us find the O'Brien woman."

I nodded and put the card in the pocket of my cutoffs. "Sure."

"Or if you decide to leave St. Thomas," Kelley said.

"Okay," I said. *Don't hold your breath waiting for that call, asshole.*

I stepped into the cockpit, and Kelley stayed on the side deck, waving for the RB-S to pick him up.

"Everything looks good, skipper. I found your vessel documentation on the chart table, so I just need your signature." The senior man handed me his clipboard.

I scrawled my name at the bottom.

"I think we got everything put back like you had it," the man said, as I returned the clipboard to him. "Only thing I want to mention is, you got a lot of expired flares. You should get rid of them; they're hazardous. You should just keep the ones that are still current."

"Right," I said. "Thanks. You saw I've got them bagged up?"

"Yes, sir."

"Looking for a good place to get rid of them. That's why they're bagged. Any suggestions?"

"Some chandleries will dispose of them for you," he said.

"I'll keep that in mind."

The two of them stood. "Safe voyage, skipper," the senior man said. They stepped onto the side deck and waved the RB-S over again.

I watched them leave the anchorage, headed southwest toward Charlotte Amalie. When they were out of sight, I went below to fetch a beer. I needed to think through this Kelley thing. The coastguardsmen behaved like they were carrying out a routine, random boarding, but Special Agent Kelley didn't pass the smell test. He knew too much about my itinerary.

7

ONCE BELOW DECK, I CHECKED TO SEE HOW WELL THE TWO
coastguardsmen did at putting the boat back together after
their search. *Island Girl's* been boarded and searched by
Coasties before. They're usually good about leaving stuff the
way they found it, unless the owner irritates them.

These two were no exception. I knew what to look for, so I
could tell they went through every locker, every nook and
cranny.

The clothes that Mary left behind might cause questions.
They were too small to fit me, even if I were to play the part of a
cross-dresser. The two men were trained professionals. I'm sure
they didn't miss Mary's stuff. Not just clothes, but typical
female things.

Would they remark on that to Kelley? Sure they would. He
might be dumb, but not that dumb. He would ask if they found
signs of another person living on the boat. So he might not buy
the story that she didn't come with me to St. Thomas.

Thanks to the tip-off from my old boss earlier, I knew the
feds were looking for Mary in connection with the slaughter in
Ste. Anne. Kelley tied her to the murder of the Daileys back in

Florida, but he didn't say anything about the bloodbath on Frankie Dailey's yacht in Ste. Anne. I wasn't naïve enough to think Special Agent Kelley was finished with me.

I considered ditching Mary's stuff. I kept it until now, figuring she would be back, but she knew the score. She wouldn't be upset if I tossed it. At this point, though, that might cause more trouble than just hanging on to it. Kelley already knew it was aboard.

There were things about Kelley that didn't add up. He called me Jerome Finnegan. That was the name I adopted when Mary and I went underground after her trouble in Bequia. It also matched the U.S. Coast Guard Certificate of Documentation for *Carib Princess*.

Both pieces of information were on the paperwork I filled out when I cleared into the U.S. with customs and immigration in St. John yesterday. They also tied back to my outbound clearance paperwork from Ste. Anne, Martinique, and Rodney Bay, St. Lucia.

But they didn't match what was in the official records in Bequia. Mary and I cleared in there with passports in different names. The vessel documentation I used was for *Island Girl*, not *Carib Princess*. Mary was using the identity of Mary Elizabeth O'Brien then. And that's what Kelley called her this morning.

When we went on the run after her problem in Bequia, I started using the Jerome Edward Finnegan passport. I also got Mary a new U.S. passport in the name of Mary Helen Maloney.

At that point, *Island Girl* became *Carib Princess*. *Island Girl* was owned by a Delaware corporation, so none of my names showed up on that Certificate of Documentation. But *Carib Princess* was owned by Jerome Finnegan. That was confusing. It was meant to be confusing.

Kelley should have expected to find Jerome Finnegan on *Carib Princess* this morning. And he should have expected that

Mary was using the Mary Helen Maloney name. That was if he
got his information legitimately.

Instead, he found me — answering to Jerome Finnegan —
on a boat bearing the name *Island Girl*. That wouldn't match
any data he had, and he didn't remark on it. So Kelley must
have found the boat's location independent of the name on her
transom.

There were several ways to explain that, but the most
straightforward was also the most disturbing. There was a
satellite tracker hidden on the boat. I knew that, but Kelley
shouldn't have, unless he was connected to the Dailey-
O'Hanlon mob.

Before I killed Frankie Dailey, he confessed that his goons
hid the tracking device aboard when they tried to kidnap Mary
in Bequia. That was how Frankie found Mary and me in Ste.
Anne.

Based on all the effort I put into covering my trail, I
suspected that Kelley must know about the tracker. That would
explain how he knew our itinerary after we left Bequia. It also
explained how he found the boat in Christmas Cove, St.
Thomas, with a different name on her transom.

The unsettling thing about that was that I thought only two
people knew about the tracker — Frankie, and me. Frankie's
dead, and I didn't tell Kelley about the tracker.

Frankie could have told one of his cohorts about the tracker.
So Kelley could have gotten our itinerary from whoever Frankie
was working for.

But most of Frankie's cohorts died in Ste. Anne, when they
made the mistake of tangling with Mary. So Kelley was in touch
with them back then. Or he was working with somebody else
who knew the story about Mary and the Daileys and Rory
O'Hanlon. That was possible, too. That would mean Kelley was
connected to someone high in the hierarchy of O'Hanlon's
old mob.

My client said Frankie was a confidential informant for the FBI. That might explain how Kelley found me, except for two things. First, I didn't believe Frankie was an informant. It didn't make sense. And second, Kelley acted wrong. Maybe he was just a jerk, but he should have played straight with me. He had no reason not to, and he didn't do that.

The bits and pieces of information I picked up from Mary argued against Frankie's cooperating with the FBI. Mary's story was convoluted, but she shared a lot of information about the Daileys and O'Hanlon during our time together.

Early in our friendship, she told me a bunch of lies. I don't blame her for that; it took her a while to decide to trust me. Then she began to tell me the truth. The parts she told me that I thought were true matched the parts that Frankie told me when I interrogated him right before I killed him.

Frankie's parents, the Daileys, were laundering drug money for his uncle, Rory O'Hanlon. O'Hanlon was Frankie's mother's brother — Frankie's uncle. Frankie caught his parents skimming and ratted them out to his uncle.

O'Hanlon hired Mary to kill Frankie's parents. As part of the package, Mary was supposed to recover the mob's money and a lot of incriminating records. Mary, being Mary, recovered everything and kept it for herself. It was more complicated than that, but that was close enough.

Frankie and his uncle tracked Mary and me, her somewhat unwitting accomplice, to Ste. Anne. They snatched her, planning to force her to turn everything over to them. They forgot how good Mary is at what they hired her to do in the first place, and she killed the lot of them.

Mary vanished and left me to deal with Frankie, who came to pick me up and take me to O'Hanlon after they snatched Mary.

I was good at what Mary does for a living, too. As I mentioned before, we were in the same business, just working for different people. After Frankie answered a few questions, I fed him to the fish.

His story and Mary's matched. Frankie was far too dirty to be sharing information with the FBI; he had too much to gain by sticking with O'Hanlon.

Kelley knew about the tracker Frankie's troops planted on *Island Girl*. Knowing about the tracker probably meant Kelley was working with the Daileys and O'Hanlon.

From the hints that Mary gave me, it was possible that O'Hanlon had a silent partner — somebody high in the government ranks. I didn't mean Kelley; he was small fry, but he could be working for that high-level silent partner.

It was time for me to move *Island Girl*; Kelley might come back. I could have gotten rid of the tracking device, but I decided to keep it.

Kelley didn't know I knew about it, so I might be able to use it to my advantage. I wasn't going to make it too easy for him, though. I planned to move outside his jurisdiction, for a start.

In an hour, I would be in the British Virgin Islands, where life would be more complicated for Special Agent Kelley. He could still find me, but he couldn't touch me without leaving an embarrassing paper trail. If I was right and he was a crook, he wouldn't do that. Maybe he would send hired help, but that was a different game — one I could play as well as he could.

8

AFTER A BRISK, TWO-HOUR SAIL FROM CHRISTMAS COVE TO Soper's Hole, Tortola, I cleared into the BVI with Her Majesty's Customs. I settled for the night in an uncrowded anchorage off Fort Recovery, near the west end of Tortola. Soper's Hole was crowded; looking for privacy, I moved around the corner after securing my clearance.

The anchorage wasn't as well protected as others nearby; it was open to the ocean swell, so it wasn't used much. *Island Girl* was rolling a lot, but she was the only boat there. That's a rare thing in the BVI, and it meant that if anybody came looking, I would spot them.

There was a nice view from my cockpit. I sipped a beer while looking across the Drake Channel at St. John, in the U.S. Virgins. U.S. territory was only a little over a mile away, but I was in the British Overseas Territory of the Virgin Islands, where FBI agents are foreigners.

Kelley could look, but that was about all he could do without getting tangled in red tape. That's been a source of frustration for law enforcement for a long time. These islands have been a smuggler's haven since before there was a United

States. Interestingly, the British Virgin Islands have a low crime rate, at least for the Caribbean. The U.S.V.I. is far more dangerous.

The Virgin Islands have always been a major transshipment point for illegal drugs and other contraband. The U.S.V.I. are a gateway to the U.S. market for illegal narcotics. Smuggling them in from the B.V.I. is easy enough for locals in tiny boats.

There's a cooperation agreement that allows U.S. law enforcement to pursue drug smugglers into the waters of the B.V.I. Casual "courtesy boardings" by the U.S. Coast Guard aren't covered by that arrangement.

If Special Agent Kelley decided to come calling again, he would have to do so as a civilian, or he would have to go through a lot of bureaucratic paperwork. If he were crooked, he wouldn't want the paper trail. I was insulated from him, at least for the moment.

I sent an encrypted text to my client while I was on my way over from Christmas Cove. She mentioned earlier that our "relatives" were looking for Mary. I debated whether to let her know one of those relatives tried to question me.

I didn't want to delay my mission, and having the FBI on my tail might have done that. But I didn't like crooks in law enforcement. It rubbed me the wrong way. I've spent my adult life in service to my country, albeit in a way that most people might think strange. And I was sure Kelley was crooked.

My client could gather background information on Kelley, and that was one reason I decided to involve her. The other reason was to cover my backside. The mission came first. If Kelley got in the way, he would suffer collateral damage at my hands. Should that happen, a record of the fact that he was sticking his nose where it didn't belong would mitigate whatever I might do to him. With advance knowledge, my client could cover for me, if it suited her needs.

There was a ping from below deck — the sound of a text

coming in to my smartphone. That wouldn't be my client; we only communicated using the special satellite phone. Not very many people knew the number for my smartphone. The last person who called or texted me was Mary, after she took off in Martinique.

Excited, I scrambled down the companionway and grabbed the phone from the drawer under the chart table. I keyed in my unlock code and went to the text messaging app. There was a message from a number I didn't recognize.

Respond if you can. No names or identifiers.

I responded with a simple *okay.*

There was an immediate reply.

Use a web browser and your VPN. Go to first boatname@youre-mail.com. Initials from my maiden name, year we met. Look in drafts folder. Delete this text. Don't respond to this number.

I erased the message and put the phone away. Opening the lid of the chart table, I took out my laptop and went back up into the cockpit. Powering up the laptop, I found an open WiFi network. I signed into a secure VPN and followed the directions from the text, sure it was from Mary. Who else could it have been?

I got as far as the password request by using the account name "islandgirl" and the server name for my regular email account after the @. For the password, I tried "meo'b2017," and I was in. I wasn't sure that was Mary's "maiden name," but it was obviously what she meant. I navigated to the drafts folder and found one message.

Hi. Miss you. Still moving fast, cleaning up after those wayward "friends" of mine. Thought we could use this for a blind email drop. After you read this, delete the draft and leave your response in the drafts folder. I'll check it when I can and leave you a response. You do the same. Stay well.

It was Mary, and just when I wished I could ask her some questions. I tapped out a quick email.

Glad you're okay. Thanks for letting me know. I have it from a trusted source that the FBI is after the woman who killed the Daileys. Your not-brother the fighter told me his troops put a tracker on the boat after you got away when they tried to snatch you that time down island. Must be how they found us. Also, there's an FBI agent in St. Thomas who knows about the tracker. He's gotta be crooked. Only way he could know is from brother dear, or someone else in the family. Did Uncle O. have partners? Need you to check the records from the family business and get word back to me ASAP. Stay well, and see you soon in our usual place, I hope.

I put the message in the drafts folder and logged out of the email account. After I closed down the laptop and stowed it, I checked the satellite phone on the off chance that my client responded to my earlier message. I was surprised to see a message waiting.

Target is in St. Barth, on a motor yacht named Witch Hunt. He has her under term charter for three months. Plans to cruise the Leewards and Windwards. Suspect he's shuffling dark money around, if that helps. Have a go ASAP, but mind the collateral damage.

Received your query re: George Kelley. Following up is taking time. Be cautious with him until you hear from us with details on how he's related.

Mind the collateral damage, she said, about Nash. In other words, she didn't want me to blow up the yacht, or kill the crew. But she wanted Nash out of the picture, and in a hurry.

I didn't tell her about the tracker on *Island Girl*, but it could be a problem. I didn't need Kelley tracking me to St. Barth. Nor was I ready to ditch the tracker. The longer I thought about it, the more curious I was to see who would follow me.

But I didn't want to find out until I took care of Nash/Nasser. Maybe I would leave *Island Girl* in Tortola and fly to St. Martin. I could charter a boat there and carry out my mission while Kelley wondered where I was.

Opening the drawer under the chart table, I took out the laptop again. I could reserve marina space and charter another yacht online.

Making airline reservations would be more risky. My online activity was anonymous, thanks to the VPN. But airline reservation systems are notoriously leaky where the feds are concerned.

A few minutes later, I was done. There would be a slip waiting for *Island Girl* the next morning in Soper's Hole. A low-rent bareboat charter company was expecting Jacob G. Finnerty to pick up a 35-foot Beneteau in St. Martin that next afternoon. A quick look at the airline schedules showed that there were plenty of puddle-jumper flights to choose from.

Since I was online, I checked the email drop. To my surprise, I found an answer from Mary. She must have been waiting and watching. That thought made me smile.

So happy to be in touch. I don't have ready access to the family records, but unless you ditched my stuff, you can help yourself. Feel along the seams in the backpack. There's a microSD card stitched in there with duplicates of everything. You're right — Uncle O could well have a partner or two still in the game. Suspect he was tight with someone in the government; no surprise there. Seeing signs of it myself. Good luck, and stay safe.

I deleted the draft from Mary and left one of my own, short and to the point.

Thanks. You too.

9

I WAS ADJUSTING TO THE FEEL OF A STRANGE BOAT. *BEST OFFER* was a modern, lightweight design; she didn't respond to the controls like *Island Girl*. It was a challenge to hold my position in the pack of boats waiting for the drawbridge opening. This was the last opening of the day. Everybody wanted out of the lagoon at St. Martin. I already put in a full day, and I was still facing two hours of sailing upwind before I reached St. Barth.

I was feeling lucky, though. Everything fell into place this morning. I tucked *Island Girl* away in the marina at Soper's Hole and got to the airport in time for a mid-morning flight to St. Martin.

After I did the paperwork to charter *Best Offer* and cleared out with customs, I stopped in a chandlery and picked up a satellite tracking device. They were easy to get and inexpensive. People used them to let friends and relatives back home track their adventures.

I intended to attach it to David Nash's yacht. If my luck held, I might catch him by himself in Gustavia, St. Barth. Then I could take care of him on the spot and relax, but I wasn't counting on it. I figured I probably used up my quota of dumb luck for one day. The tracker would expand my options.

My client said Nash planned to cruise the islands for a while. There were better places for me to kill him than St. Barth. It would be crowded, and the French police there were better organized than their colleagues in the Eastern Caribbean countries.

With a tracker on *Witch Hunt*, I could choose where to kill Nash. I didn't yet know what kind of vessel *Witch Hunt* was, but the client said she was a motor yacht. She would certainly be faster than *Best Offer*. Once I planted the device, I could sail on down island and let Nash come to me, so boat speed wouldn't be an issue.

I could have chartered a powerboat, but that would have attracted more attention than a generic chartered sailboat. *Best Offer* was almost identical to the hundreds of her sister ships that made up the bareboat charter fleets in the islands.

Some were a little larger; a few were smaller, but they were all white, no-frills boats with blue canvas. They were everywhere, and the people sailing them were often unskilled, so I'd have to do something awfully strange to attract attention.

Even if there weren't a tracking device on *Island Girl*, I would have chartered because of the anonymity it gave me. Plus, *Best Offer* was almost disposable. If I needed to make a quick getaway, I could leave her where she sat and call the charter company to pick her up when it was convenient for them. She was like a floating rental car.

The drawbridge opened on time, and I joined the parade of boats exiting the lagoon. It was a good bet that half of them were going to St. Barth. It was close by and a popular spot for charterers. That suited me. I would be less obvious as part of the pack.

Leaving St. Martin that time of day, we would reach St. Barth in daylight. Still, it would be too late to clear in with the authorities. The French were easy-going when it came to the formalities of customs and immigration, at least for visiting yachts. That made the French islands good vacation destinations. I could handle my inbound clearance in the morning, if I decided to stay.

If I managed to plant my tracker that evening, I planned to move on in the morning. As I mentioned, there were better places for me to deal with David Nash.

Once through the drawbridge and out in Simpson Bay, I set the autopilot to hold the bow into the wind while I unfurled the mainsail. I didn't like roller-furling sails on an ocean-going boat, but they sure made it easy for a single-hander. The course to St. Barth was too close to the wind to sail, but the mainsail caught enough wind to steady the boat. In a hurry to get there, I powered into the choppy swell with the auxiliary diesel engine.

With the sail up and sheeted in tight, I adjusted my course as I rounded Pelican Point. Headed straight for St. Barth, I was able to trim the sail so it wasn't flogging. I re-engaged the autopilot and adjusted the throttle to keep my speed at *Best Offer's* upper limit.

I was right; almost half the boats that came through the drawbridge with me were on course for St. Barth. I kept an eye on my neighbors until we were spread out enough to avoid collisions. Then I ducked below and retrieved my laptop.

Back in the cockpit, I found a shady spot under the dodger so I could read the screen. After I retrieved Mary's microSD card last night, I copied all the files to a folder on my hard drive. Then I put the card back in its hiding place. This was my first chance to look at the files.

I was astonished at how much information could be packed into a few hundred megabytes. The files weren't in any rational order that I could recognize. There were quite a few folders, and loads of files mixed in among them. The file names didn't tell me much. Some were date ranges, some were place names.

There was a mix of file types: Word, Excel, PDF, plain text, html. The same was true of the folder names, and their contents were mixed, too.

I navigated back out to the folder I copied the files into. I left it with the default name — "new folder" when I copied the files into it. Even though my computer was encrypted, I tried to avoid making it easy for anyone to find their way around my stuff.

All my data folders were named "new folder." The machine assigned a number following the name. This one's "new folder (37)." I would remember that so I could get back to it, but to a stranger, even one who got past the encryption, it wouldn't mean much.

I checked the metadata for "new folder (37)" and learned that it contained 3,852 files and 113 folders. My head started to ache, just thinking about it. I was too tired to even begin to devise a plan for an organized search. Wondering if Mary had a clue as to how the files were organized, I shook my head.

I shut down the computer and took a couple of minutes to watch the other boats. We were spread out comfortably — nothing to worry about. I picked up the computer and took it below, putting it away.

Filling a kettle with water, I clamped it in place on the stovetop. Then I released the latch that locked the stove in place. Allowing the stove to swing in its gimbals as the boat rocked kept the water from sloshing out of the kettle. I lit the burner and spooned instant coffee into a vacuum bottle I found in one of the galley lockers.

I expected to have a long night ahead of me, and while the boats nearby weren't uncomfortably close, there was too much traffic for me to risk napping. The coffee would keep me going until I anchored in St. Barth. By the time I scouted the harbor and planted my tracker on *Witch Hunt*, I'd be tired enough to sleep despite the caffeine.

As I expected, it was about a half hour before sundown by the time I got *Best Offer* anchored in the outer harbor at Gustavia, St. Barth. It was crowded, but that wasn't unusual. Using a spare halyard, I hoisted the rigid inflatable boat that was stowed on the foredeck.

When it was swinging free and high enough to clear the lifelines, I unwrapped the halyard from the winch drum, leaving one turn. By pulling hard on the tail of the halyard with my left hand, I kept the RIB in the air. Throwing my weight into it, I gave the RIB a shove to swing it out over the water. I let the halyard run free, and the RIB landed with a splash.

I climbed down into it and unhooked the halyard, refastening it to the base of the lifeline stanchion. Hand over hand, I walked the RIB around to *Best Offer's* transom and tied it there. A 15-horsepower outboard was clamped to the stern rail, with a little hand-operated crane to raise and lower it. After jockeying the RIB into position so that its stern was directly below the outboard, I climbed up into *Best Offer's* cockpit and lowered the outboard.

Retrieving the outboard's fuel tank from where it was stashed under the helmsman's seat, I climbed back down into the RIB and finished mounting the outboard. Connecting the fuel line, I crossed my fingers and pulled the starter handle. I was relieved when the engine sputtered to life on my second try.

I untied the lines holding the RIB to *Best Offer* and motored into Gustavia's inner harbor in search of *Witch Hunt*. A few minutes later, I spotted her. She was one of several big motor vessels moored stern-to the seawall in the marina.

Witch Hunt wasn't remarkable among her neighbors. She was neither the largest nor the smallest of the big motor yachts docked there. Typically, her stern was several feet out from the seawall, with a gangway running up from her swim platform to the concrete abutment. She was held away from the wall by two

anchors run out from her bow, their chains making a "V" with
an angle of about 45 degrees. Hawsers ran from her stern to
massive bollards set atop the seawall. A gap of several feet separated her from the vessels on either side. Big pneumatic fenders
hung along the sides to protect the yachts from bumping one
another if the wind kicked up.

There was no sign of anyone aboard, but that didn't mean
much. *Witch Hunt* was between 120 and 140 feet in length.
There was a lot of smoked glass in her superstructure, affording
a good view of the harbor to anyone concealed behind it. I kept
moving, careful to study all the big boats. I gawked like a
tourist, in case somebody was watching.

Once I made the rounds of the harbor, I headed back to *Best
Offer*. I would return in the wee hours of the morning to plant
my tracking device. Gustavia's a spot that offers nightlife; I
would have to be careful. Wandering drunks didn't worry me,
but they might keep Nash's security team on high alert.

Tying the RIB to *Best Offer's* stern, I climbed the boarding
ladder into the cockpit. It was time for dinner and a long nap.

10

STARTLED BY THE RINGING, I FUMBLED FOR MY IPHONE AND answered it, half asleep. Then I remembered setting the alarm; it wasn't a phone call. I had some tests to run on the tracker I was going to plant on *Witch Hunt.*

Rubbing my eyes, I turned on my laptop and went online. I set up an account for the tracking device and verified that it was working. For my testing, I set the update interval on the tracker for five minutes.

I put a pot of coffee on to perk. When it finished, I logged in to the web page for the satellite tracker. Navigating to the link I created earlier, I saw the blinking dot that marked the tracker's location. Hovering the cursor over the blinking dot for a second brought up a block of text with the latitude and longitude of my current location. The speed of the tracker was zero knots. A course was displayed, but it was meaningless in this case, since the device wasn't moving.

I wrote down the location and logged off, then poured myself a cup of coffee. Eleven minutes later, I logged in again and got an updated position. Although the tracker was still on the chart table, *Best Offer* had moved, swinging on her anchor, so I saw updated position information.

Zooming in, I saw a series of three plot points, almost stacked on top of one another. The most recent showed an updated course that matched our track as we swung to the anchor, and a speed of -0.1 knots. My tracker was working.

Satisfied that I configured the device properly, I adjusted its update interval to 30 minutes instead of five. Thirty-minute updates would give two weeks of battery life, according to the instructions. If I couldn't kill Nash in two weeks, I would need another plan anyway.

I drank the rest of my coffee and put on my wetsuit. Stuffing the tracker into a waterproof pouch at my waist, I gathered the rest of my gear and went up into the cockpit. A quick look around satisfied me that no one was visible on the neighboring boats, so I put on my mask and flippers and slipped into the water.

Earlier, I thought of taking *Best Offer's* RIB at least part of the way to *Witch Hunt*, but I rejected the idea. There were places to leave the RIB along the way, but there was too much chance that someone might see me slipping into the water in my wetsuit and snorkeling gear.

Snorkeling at three o'clock in the morning was unusual enough to attract attention. From where I anchored *Best Offer*, it was only a quarter mile to the megayacht dock at the marina. I decided it was safer to swim. In an all-black wetsuit with a hood, black equipment, and camouflage paint on my exposed skin, I was close to invisible.

I drifted along for a moment to get my bearings and then started swimming. Out in the anchorage, there was enough chop so that I didn't have to worry about splashing, so I was making good time. I would slow down when I felt the chop diminish.

11

THE HIGH-PITCHED WHINE IN MY EARS GREW LOUDER BY THE second. From experience, I knew the sound was coming from a good-sized outboard, and it was moving fast. I stopped swimming and raised my head out of the water, looking toward the marina.

Seeing no moving boats, I turned, treading water. A big RIB was approaching the harbor entrance. It was probably a tender to one of the large crewed charter yachts in the outer anchorage, going to pick up passengers who were visiting the nightclubs in Gustavia.

I watched for a few seconds, making sure that I wasn't in their path. The RIB passed 200 yards south of me. Before I put my face back in the water, I raised my left wrist and glanced at my watch. After swimming for ten minutes, I was maybe five minutes from *Witch Hunt*.

I kicked with my fins and put my face down, resuming my swim. From the flat water I was swimming through two minutes later, I could tell that I was well inside the inner harbor. I glided to a stop and raised my head again, moving slowly to avoid being spotted. I was about fifty yards off the bow of the first big motoryacht that was moored stern-to. *Witch Hunt* was the third one in.

I saw a dark figure standing on her bow, looking out at the small boats on the mooring balls. A sentry? Maybe so. I watched for a full minute, long enough to see the person take a last drag on a cigarette and flick it out into the harbor.

The figure turned and mounted a set of stairs leading up to the bridge. There was low-level lighting on the stairs, and I could see that this was a man dressed in white, like paid crew. He could still have been a security guard, though. And it didn't matter anyway. I couldn't let anyone see me. There was no innocent explanation for what I was about to do.

I took several deep breaths, hyperventilating, and dove, swimming underwater toward the bow of *Witch Hunt*. The water was clear and only about twelve feet deep, so I stayed close to the bottom. There was enough ambient light to make me nervous; somebody who was watching fish might see me.

I found a pair of heavy anchor chains a few feet apart, hanging in the water. Their weight pulled them into a catenary that was almost vertical where they broke the surface.

That close to the big yachts, I was hidden from anyone standing on deck. I followed one chain to the surface and verified that I was under *Witch Hunt's* bow. I put my hand on the mouthpiece of my snorkel and took it from between my teeth, letting the water drain from it. Blowing through it to clear it in the normal way would have given me away if anyone were on deck.

I hung on the chain and caught my breath while I considered where to affix the tracker. *Witch Hunt* was an ultramodern design with lots of curved surfaces. I found the style unattractive, but it did offer several places to conceal a tracking device.

The tracker would work best with an unobstructed view of the sky, so the top surface of the tip of the bow was a good spot. When I scouted earlier, I saw that the point of the bow was rounded at the top, and it was finished in brilliant white gelcoat.

That was a perfect place for the tracking device. A few inches behind the spot I picked out, there was a short jackstaff where a yacht club burgee was flying in the breeze. The burgee would block the tracker from casual view.

When I bought the tracker, I picked up a few other items. Two aerosol cans of quick-drying lacquer would make the device less noticeable when it was installed. One was glossy white, the other a glossy medium brown, in case I needed to mount the device on varnished wood.

A pack of industrial grade, double-faced foam mounting tape solved the problem of how to fasten the tracker to *Witch Hunt*. When I got back to the boat earlier, after my recon run in the dinghy, I sprayed the tracker with the white paint and stuck a piece of mounting tape on the back.

All I needed to do was climb to where I could reach the tip of the bow, peel the backing off the foam tape and stick the tracker in place. The anchor chain was easy enough to climb, but that left several feet of slick, glossy fiberglass for me to traverse to get to where I needed to be.

Removing my mask, snorkel, and fins, I threaded them onto a short length of parachute cord and tied them to the anchor chain where it broke the surface. I was already wearing neoprene dive gloves and booties, both perfect for climbing the chain without losing any skin.

Wrapping my legs around the chain, I reached up as far as I could and grasped the chain with both hands, pulling with my arms and pushing with my legs. Careful not to go too fast and rattle the chain, I spent almost a minute reaching the hawse pipe where the anchor chain came through the side of the hull.

Holding on with my legs and one hand, I opened my belt pack and took out a set of the big suction cups sold in chandleries. They were used by divers for holding on while scrubbing the bottom of a boat. They were also used to pick up sheets of plate glass around construction sights ashore.

Reaching up, I stuck one suction cup in place and pulled, working my way up the chain with my feet. Sticking the second suction cup in place, I was able to climb high enough to put a foot in the hawse pipe. By straightening my leg, I could reach up and over to where I wanted to put the tracker.

I took the tracker from my belt pack with my free hand and brought it up to my mouth. Anticipating this, I freed a corner of the backing on the mounting tape earlier. I clamped the backing paper corner between my teeth and pulled it off. Straightening my leg again, I pressed the tracker in place and pulled on it to test its grip.

Satisfied it would stay there, I used the thumb lever on the higher suction cup to release it. After another minute of working my way down the chain, I was back in the water. I retrieved my snorkeling gear, put it on, and used the chain to pull myself down to the bottom of the lagoon.

I swam under water until I was in the middle of the mooring field where the smaller boats were secured. Surfacing for a breath, I got my bearings before I ducked back under the surface and swam toward the harbor entrance. I held my breath until I was far enough from all the moored boats to swim on the surface without the risk of being seen.

I took my time; there were a few people walking along the waterfront — early risers, or late drunks. I didn't want to splash and call attention to myself. Soon, I was back aboard *Best Offer*. Before I took off my gear, I went below and powered up the laptop.

After I satisfied myself that the tracker was working, I shut down the computer and cleaned myself up. My swim to *Witch Hunt* took an hour. It was four a.m.; I would nap for a few hours and then get underway. There was no reason to stay in St. Barth any longer.

12

IT WAS A BEAUTIFUL MORNING. I WAS ROLLING ALONG UNDER FULL sail, making seven knots on a direct course to Antigua. *Best Offer* was in her element; she was on a close reach in 15 knots of wind.

We left St. Barth an hour ago. At this rate, we would arrive in Antigua a little after dark. I decided on Antigua for a couple of reasons. One, if Nash were "shuffling dark money around," as my client put it in her text, Antigua was a likely spot. It was by no means the only one, but it also put me out to the east with a good angle on the trade winds to sail down island. That was my other reason.

The autopilot was doing a good job holding the course, and there was not another boat in sight. I went below and put a kettle on the stove; it was time for some coffee. While it perked, I took out the sat phone and my laptop. Reaching through the companionway, I set the computer and the phone on the bridge deck.

I spent another few minutes plotting a position on the paper chart I found in the chart drawer. There was no real need, but it was something to do while I waited for my coffee.

Once the water was hot, I made a mug of instant and put it on the bridge deck next to the other stuff. I used the rest of the hot water to make a thermos of coffee for later.

Climbing back into the cockpit, I stood up and scanned the horizon. There were still no other vessels in sight. That was nice; I was enjoying the solitude. I took a sip of coffee and powered up the laptop. There was no internet service out here, but I made a note of the link to the tracking website, along with the user name and password I set up.

With that information on the screen, I picked up the satellite phone and keyed it in. I shut off the computer and finished composing a text to my client, telling her what I was up to. It wasn't required, but it was good business. If she wanted to, she could track *Witch Hunt* herself to keep up with Nash. Besides, at some point, she would have to approve the expense for this junket. *Best Offer* might be like a floating rental car, but she cost quite a bit more.

With the text sent, I considered powering on the laptop again and trying to make sense of Mary's files. Then I got distracted by two dolphins putting on a show off the starboard quarter. There would be time to look at the files later.

I was sipping coffee and smiling at the dolphins when the satellite phone rang. Stunned, I put the coffee down and reached for the phone. As I said, no one could call it except my client, and she rarely did.

Answering an incoming call wasn't as simple as on a normal sat phone. I went through the series of codes and voice recognition screening, and then I heard her voice.

"I hope I'm not interrupting. Is this a convenient time for us to talk about your request from the other day?"

She was giving me time to recognize her voice, and an opportunity to excuse myself if I didn't happen to be in a position to talk freely.

"Yes."

"You recognize my voice?"

"Yes. I just sent you a text."

"I got it. That's why I thought this would be a good time to talk. Are you at sea?"

"Yes. I won't be at my destination for several hours. Not until after dark."

"About your request, then. I'm not sure what you've stumbled into. You know who my boss is?"

I hesitated; I wasn't supposed to know that, but she was my boss for a long time. A guy like me figured out stuff like that. It was one of the skills that made me suited for the job. And a woman like her knew that. But I was shocked at the question, just the same. I decided to be honest with her.

"Yes. I mean, not by name, but — "

"Okay," she interrupted me. "That's enough. My boss just got an ass-chewing about a request for super-sensitive personnel information coming out of our department. You know what I'm talking about?"

"I think so. If I'm right, apologize on my behalf."

"Not necessary. People are pissed off, all right, but not at us."

Her boss was an undersecretary reporting to the Secretary of Defense. The position didn't show up on any organization charts. I didn't know anything about the person in the job — man, woman, old, young. Only my boss and the Secretary of Defense knew.

We were a small operation as government entities went. My boss's boss was the highest level who wasn't politically vulnerable. I wasn't sure how that worked, but I suspected there was some fear instilled in the upper echelons of the chain of command. Crossing my boss's boss would be dangerous.

"Who's your boss upset with, then?"

"The asshole who chewed out the Secretary."

Damn, she was good. She told me what I needed to know and nothing more, all in an innocuous sentence. Anybody who overheard her would picture a middle-aged woman with a steno pad getting raked over the coals. Only my client and I knew who the asshole was. There was only one person who could chew out the Secretary of Defense.

"You know what I mean?"

"Yes," I said, thinking my way through this. Special Agent George Kelley had high-level protection. "What do you want me to do?" I was braced for her answer, but life was full of surprises.

"Take care of your mission first. Then we'll figure out how to find the culprit and exact retribution. I'm assuming you want in on this. If you want to play the retirement card, I understand."

"I'm in."

"I knew you would be."

"I guess this is all you learned from the inquiry, huh?"

"Don't underestimate the people you're reporting to. There's more than one way to skin a pol — a cat."

I laughed. "Pol-a-cat? Polecats can stink when you upset them."

"Yeah. Damn skunks and politicians both. Tell me about it. Take care of your end."

With that, she was gone. I put the phone down and picked up my lukewarm coffee. I needed to give Mary a heads-up, without breaching national security. At least I would have several hours to think about that before I could get online and leave her a message.

13

THE SUN WAS JUST PEEKING OVER THE ISLAND OF ANTIGUA. THE anchorage outside the Jolly Harbour entrance was still in shadow when I brought my first coffee of the day up into the cockpit. The customs and immigration office wouldn't be open for two hours, but I knew there was public WiFi available out here in the anchorage.

I took a sip of my coffee and opened the laptop. I could kill an hour here and then go in for breakfast at the restaurant in the marina. By then, the customs office would be open and I could clear in.

Once connected, I checked on *Witch Hunt's* position. Nash was moving; *Witch Hunt* was about two hours away, moving toward Antigua at 15 knots. Given their speed, they left St. Barth sometime early this morning. My guess about Antigua as their first stop was correct. I would have to wait and see which harbor they chose, but I was betting on Falmouth Harbour.

English Harbour was also a possibility, but it was far more touristy than Falmouth. Nash wouldn't be here for sightseeing; Falmouth was much more business-like and less crowded. Either would accommodate *Witch Hunt.* Jolly Harbour would, as well, but a boat that size would attract too much attention in Jolly Harbour.

Finished with my coffee, I logged in to the blind drop email account that Mary and I were using. I left her a message last night warning her that the FBI agent I mentioned earlier was corrupt, and that his friends in high places were covering for him.

I didn't tell her how high. It didn't matter, for now, and I was curious to see how she would respond. I would have to wait, though. The message I left for her was still sitting in the drafts folder. She must have been busy.

I closed the laptop and picked up the satellite phone. I figured I might as well give my boss an update on Nash. Knowing he was headed for Antigua, she could research whether he had contacts in the financial community there. Anything she discovered might be useful.

With that message composed and sent, I poured another mug of coffee and turned my thoughts to the day ahead. I would stick to my plan of breakfast and customs clearance at Jolly Harbour. By the time I was done, *Witch Hunt* should be arriving.

Once I knew where she was berthed, I would move to her neighborhood and begin surveillance. Given that Nash was probably here to meet somebody, he would most likely be going ashore. The banks were in downtown St. John, the capital city.

That would mean ground transportation for Nash, so I would find myself an inconspicuous spot ashore where I could watch for him. All I needed was a split second of inattention on his part. Getting into or out of a car would do.

It was late enough for me to move in to the customs dock. I put everything away and fired up the diesel, leaving it to idle while I rigged fenders and dock lines. That done, I went up to the foredeck and retrieved the anchor, enjoying the luxury of an electric anchor windlass. Maybe someday, I would install one on *Island Girl*.

I pulled in alongside the customs dock and tied *Best Offer* up at the outside end. Being alone, I didn't want other boats to block me in. Tied at the outer end, I could cast off the lines and back straight out after I handled the formalities.

I gathered my paperwork and locked the companionway before I climbed onto the dock. Walking to the seawall, I followed the sidewalk a hundred yards or so to the south. I pulled up a stool at the snack bar there and ordered scrambled eggs and saltfish patties.

Once I ate and drank another cup of coffee, I strolled back to the customs office. The agent was still getting her desk set up, but she greeted me and pushed a form across the counter. Ten minutes later, I was back aboard *Best Offer*.

I unlocked the companionway and went below, stashing the paperwork in the chart table. Firing up the laptop, I clicked my way to the tracking website and found that *Witch Hunt* was on course to enter Falmouth Harbour soon. If I hurried, I could be there shortly after she settled into a berth.

Back up on deck, I retrieved the dock lines. I looped them around the cleats on the dock when I came in, bringing the ends of the lines back aboard *Best Offer* to tie them. That was a single-hander's trick. It enabled me to untie the lines from the cleats on *Best Offer's* toe rail and pull the lines back aboard without setting foot on the dock.

Dropping the lines on deck, I went back to the helm and engaged reverse gear, opening the throttle a bit. *Best Offer* backed away from the dock, and I shifted to neutral, letting her coast backward. The breeze blew the bow around so it pointed to the northeast.

When *Best Offer* was about 100 feet from the dock, I put her in forward gear and cranked the helm around to the port, bumping the throttle open a little. The boat twirled in her own length, and I headed for the harbor entrance.

An hour and a half later, I dropped the anchor off Pigeon Beach in Falmouth Harbour. I was just south of the marked channel to the marina. *Witch Hunt* was approaching the marina's dock. She must have had to wait while they moved boats around to accommodate her. My timing was perfect.

I dropped the RIB in the water and mounted the outboard while I kept an eye on *Best Offer's* position relative to her neighbors. Satisfied that we were not going to swing into the other boats nearby, I went below and put the laptop and my phones in a canvas briefcase.

As an afterthought, I tossed in a small pair of binoculars and a compact camera with a good zoom lens. I didn't need pictures of *Witch Hunt,* but a camera would be good cover. With binoculars and a camera, I could pass myself off as a bird-watcher while I spied on Nash.

I locked up and climbed down into the dinghy. As *Witch Hunt's* crew finished securing her to the outer dock at the marina, I pulled in to the dinghy dock and clambered ashore. Now I needed to find a good vantage point and see what David Nash/Daoud Nasser was up to.

14

THE MARINA IN FALMOUTH HARBOUR INCLUDED A LARGE
building with lots of shops and restaurants. I was sitting at an
outdoor table on the balcony of a second-floor internet café
that afforded me a good view of *Witch Hunt,* maybe 50 yards
away. With my laptop open in front of me, I stayed a couple of
hours, drinking decaf espresso to pay my rent. To pass the time,
I forced myself to read through the files that Mary took from
the Daileys, but it was slow going.

An hour earlier, Nash and a guy who might as well have
worn a T-shirt with "Bodyguard" printed on it came outside.
They went to the aft deck of *Witch Hunt* and stood there. Nash
was talking and gesturing toward shore, and the other guy was
listening intently and nodding his head.

After a few minutes, Nash went back inside, and Bodyguard
came ashore and went into the rental car office across the way
from where I was sitting. He was in there for five minutes, and
then he emerged, keys in hand. I stood, pretending to stretch
the kinks from my back, and moved around the balcony far
enough to watch him go to the parking lot. He approached a
white mid-sized sedan, walking around the car and looking it

over. He opened the trunk and closed it, then headed back to *Witch Hunt.*

When Bodyguard was back on the boat, I gave the waitress who was taking care of me a few dollars to keep an eye on my computer and went downstairs. Out in the parking lot, I made sure no one was watching. Satisfied I wasn't observed, I walked past the car Bodyguard rented and bent to adjust the laces of my running shoes.

I stood up and went on my way, listening to the satisfying hiss as the car's right rear tire went flat. That might have been enough of a distraction to meet my needs, or it might have just annoyed Bodyguard. Nothing ventured, nothing gained. I went back to my table, ordering another espresso from the waitress when she greeted me.

As I drained the last of my espresso, I saw movement on *Witch Hunt.* I watched as Nash and Bodyguard came down the gangway and walked along the dock, headed toward the parking lot. Closing the lid of my laptop, I slipped it into my canvas briefcase.

I nodded at the waitress and made sure she saw me leave some bills on the table. She smiled and told me to hurry back. By the time I was downstairs and in sight of the parking lot, Bodyguard and Nash were in the car. Bodyguard was behind the wheel; Nash held a cell phone to his ear, nodding his head as he talked with someone.

Bodyguard backed out of the parking place and drove a few feet, then he stopped and got out. Walking around the car, he bent to look at the flat tire and cursed. He pulled the car back into the parking place, said something to Nash, and got out again, leaving the car running to keep the air conditioning on. Nash was still on his phone call.

I turned my back and pretended to window shop as I listened to Bodyguard's approaching footsteps. He was pissed; I could tell from the way his feet smacked the pavement.

I was standing in a little passageway that cut through the ground floor of the building that housed the shops. There were display windows on each corner of the passageway. As Bodyguard stomped past me, I turned from my window shopping, bumping into him. He cursed and shoved me, his right hand on my chest.

I trapped his hand and spun in a clockwise direction, locking his right elbow in an extended position and forcing him to a crouch. He was good; even taken by surprise, he reacted in the right way, twisting to his left to take the pressure off his elbow and hooking my left knee with his left hand.

He would have taken me down, except that I knew the move and anticipated it. I drove the ice pick in my left hand up under his chin, through his tongue and soft palette into his brain. As he convulsed, I retrieved the ice pick and wiped it on his shirt.

Halfway through the passageway, there was a door marked "Trash." I dragged the body through the door. The trash room was half-filled with black plastic bags, each bulging with garbage. I covered my victim with several of the full bags, hiding him from view. Fitting, I thought. Maybe that would buy me a little time before somebody found him.

Walking to the car, I shifted the ice pick to my right hand. Nash glanced up as I jerked the passenger door open. He turned his head to look at me, still talking on the phone. His eyes registered surprise when he saw I wasn't Bodyguard. Before he could react, I drove the icepick into his left ear, right up to the hilt. His eyes went wide, and he gasped one final breath. I pulled the ice pick out and wiped it on his shoulder, dropping it in my briefcase as I closed the car door.

At a casual pace, I walked back to the building with the shops and entered a ground-floor restaurant. It was still early enough for lunch, and my day's work was already done.

A waiter brought me a menu and gave me a card with the password for the restaurant's WiFi. He recommended the fish and chips special, so I ordered that and a Guinness. While I waited for my food, I checked the blind email drop, but the message I left for Mary last night was still there in the drafts folder.

I kept expecting to hear sirens, but it was quiet. By the time I finished my lunch, there was still no sign that anyone had found the bodies. That wasn't surprising, I guess. The place seemed dead in the middle of the day, no pun intended. But I was surprised that whoever was on the phone with Nash didn't raise an alarm. Maybe they were used to spotty cellphone service here.

I settled my check and went back to *Best Offer,* deciding to sail back to Jolly Harbour. Falmouth Harbour was a rough neighborhood; I wasn't sure it was safe to spend the night there.

15

FAR ENOUGH FROM ANTIGUA TO BE OUT OF THE ISLAND'S WIND shadow, I unfurled *Best Offer's* sails and shut down the diesel. The previous day was a busy one for me. After returning to the anchorage outside the Jolly Harbour entrance, I took the dinghy in and cleared out with customs and immigration for an early departure this morning.

I would make St. Martin around sunset. That was too late for the last drawbridge into the lagoon; the anchorage out in Simpson Bay would have to serve for the evening. I would clear in the next morning and drop the boat off at the charter company. By that night, I would be home on *Island Girl*.

Once I was settled in the anchorage off Jolly Harbour last night, I caught up on my correspondence. I sent my client a short text to let her know my mission was accomplished, and I used the public WiFi in the anchorage to check for messages from Mary.

I found a lengthy response from her in the drafts folder of our blind email drop. Relieved to hear from her, I fetched a beer from the ice box and settled in to read.

Hello, sailor!

Hope all's well in your world. Things are still messy here, but I'm making steady progress. I cleaned up several loose ends from Uncle O's estate, but the more I look, the more I find.

About that foreign-born Irish guy you mentioned — watch out for him. I got my hands on the files we were talking about. There are some references there that could explain his interest. A couple of the relatives I've talked with mentioned that there was a guy in your part of the world who was sent to find those records. He's also supposed to find my "brother." Maybe the foreign-born guy you mentioned. Still checking on that.

I'm not sure it's worth your trouble to try to make sense of those old family records. I have enough context to find my way through them, but I'm sure they're overwhelming without clues as to how they fit together. Don't worry about trying to decipher them; just make sure you have a copy in a safe place. I may need to retrieve them from you, and the family may suspect that you have them.

You never said how you got on with brother dear, but I'm guessing he was a hit with you. The family up here is missing him and his sidekick — did my brother introduce you when you were all together that time? Let me know how it went when you get a chance; I'll tell his aunt.

Meanwhile, I'm surprised at the size of the extended family. I always thought Uncle was the patriarch of the clan, but not so. Still trying to figure out how all these people are related and who's in charge.

I didn't know so many of my distant cousins were such powerful people in our government. Some of them are important enough that I'll need a little help to set up meetings with them, but it has to be done to settle the estate.

I could use your assistance, if you have time to spare. There's no big hurry; these people aren't going anywhere. Thinking maybe you and I should meet up a little sooner than we planned. We need to talk this over face-to-face, if you're available.

Let me know when you'll be free. Travel's no problem for me. I'd love to see you again. Look forward to your reply.

It took more than one beer for me to digest that. I chuckled at her use of "foreign-born Irish" to describe Kelley. I never heard the U.S. Irish Catholic slang term "FBI" used to refer to an Irish immigrant until Mary used it a few weeks ago. It amused me that she turned it around to avoid naming Kelley. She picked up something about him from contacts in the States, apparently.

Working with her appealed to me; there was no question about that. But there were risks, too. Although I was "retired," my client would take a dim view of freelance activities that made use of my special skills. And when I read between the lines, that's what Mary was hinting at. Or at least, I thought she was.

We needed that face-to-face meeting. I still wasn't sure about Mary's identity and affiliations. Before Frankie Dailey passed away, he told me she was a hired gun. That wasn't inconsistent with what I knew about her. He implied that she was in business for herself, but he wasn't the most reliable source.

Most people who guessed what I did for a living thought I was self-employed, too. I wasn't, but people in my profession worked hard to protect the identity of our employers. I wasn't trying to convince myself that Mary was a government agent of some kind, but she could well be.

Who really knew how many obscure little "departments" existed in our government? Departments that exist to solve common-sense problems that the voting public and our elected representatives chose not to know about?

I had spent too long in this game to believe my own organization was unique. I knew for a fact that it wasn't. Over the years, I ran across other people like me. More than once, our paths converged on common targets. Given our work, we didn't sit down over a drink and compare notes. But we tacitly acknowledged one another.

Sometimes, I improved the odds for one of the others. It was just another way of getting my job done. I didn't have to pull the trigger myself every time.

I didn't send Mary an answer last night, as tempting as it was. The impulsive side of my nature wanted to, but I've conditioned myself to suppress my impulses. Behavior that might be a minor embarrassment to the average person could have dire consequences for me — or for someone else.

Tonight would be soon enough to give Mary an answer. Maybe too soon. Meanwhile, I got a strange text from my client this morning as I was leaving the anchorage. The timing alone was odd; the message was sent at 3 a.m., her time.

For her to be sending messages at that time of day meant something out of the ordinary was going on. And then there was the message content, which was even more strange than the timing.

That person you asked about the other day — repercussions still coming. Tone of reaction to our request for info on him has changed. Keep him close, but be wary. Mixed messages on him. He may become a target, but not yet.

Stand by for further direction.

I was struggling to grasp her meaning. Confusion was evident in those few short sentences, but in almost 20 years of working at her direction, I never knew my client to be confused. If she ever was, she kept it to herself. So I would do what she suggested; I would stand by for further direction. I was shocked by the implication that she might want me to eliminate an FBI agent. I never heard of such a thing — executing a U.S. citizen was rare enough, but an FBI agent? Even a crooked one... Kelley must have been into something heavy.

I was having a beautiful sail while I puzzled over what to do about Mary and what to make of my client's message. Mary's request wasn't too surprising. My client's message was far more unsettling. And the fact that both of them seemed to be warning me about Special Agent George Kelley was worrisome.

Their comments and my deduction that Kelley knew about the tracker Frankie's troops put on *Island Girl* all pointed to his being crooked. That was unusual, although Kelley wouldn't be the first FBI agent who went astray.

He might work out of San Juan, or he could be assigned to the resident office in St. Thomas. Either one would make him a valuable ally for crooks smuggling drugs or people through the islands to the U.S. mainland.

Thoughts of lunch were distracting me when I heard the ping of a text message arriving on the satellite phone. It was below deck on the chart table. Standing up, I scanned the horizon for other vessels. I was all alone out there, so I engaged the autopilot. I would check the message and fix myself a sandwich or two.

Once below, I picked up the sat phone and keyed in all the codes. A text from my boss appeared, and when the implications sunk in, I felt a chill run down my spine.

This means of communications is compromised. Act accordingly. Do not attempt to initiate contact by other means.

Talk about short and to the point. I powered off the phone and used a straightened paper clip to open the SIM drawer. Removing the SIM card, I put it on the chart table while I mounted the companionway ladder. With a clear view of the horizon, I cocked my arm and launched the phone in a long, flat arc. Watching the splash when it hit the water, I swallowed hard and wondered what the hell was going on.

Back below, I pulled the tweezers from my Swiss Army knife and picked up the SIM card. Lighting a burner on the galley stove, I held the SIM card in the flame. It melted into a sooty blob and then caught fire for a few seconds.

When the flames died down, I climbed into the cockpit

with the charred drop of plastic still in the tweezers. Putting it down on the cockpit seat, I folded out the small blade on the Swiss Army knife. I picked up the tweezers again and held them over the downwind side of the boat, using the knife to scrape the charred mess off the stainless-steel tweezers.

That was overkill to get rid of the SIM card. I could have just tossed it over the side, but burning it was consistent with my training, and it gave me something to do.

Sticking the tweezers back in their slot, I closed the knife and put it in my pocket. Below deck again, I assembled sandwich makings as I wondered what would come next.

16

THE RIDE WAS WILD OUT IN THE SIMPSON BAY ANCHORAGE. *BEST Offer* was rolling through about 15 degrees to each side of vertical. A heavier displacement, old-fashioned design like *Island Girl* would still have been rolling in those conditions, but she would have been far more comfortable. It had to do with inertia. *Best Offer* was a lighter-weight boat. She started, accelerated, and stopped much more quickly than *Island Girl*. I felt like I would get whiplash every few seconds.

Sleeping in those conditions wasn't possible, at least for me. I was lying awake, holding on so I didn't get tossed from my berth. To pass the time, I thought through my situation vis-à-vis Mary and my client.

While I was sailing along with the autopilot on this afternoon, I composed a response to Mary. I kept it generic.

Glad to hear from you. I'm doing well. I've been away from Island Girl for a couple of days, but I'll be back aboard tomorrow. Don't worry about the family records; I have a copy. Your copy's where you left it.

I'm not surprised at the size of your family. Guess it's that Irish Catholic thing, huh? I've heard more rumors about that foreign-born person we were talking about. He's got an interesting background. I'll tell you more when I see you.

Speaking of getting together, my time is yours. I just finished up a little business, and I don't have anything on my agenda. Would love to see you. Time and place of your choosing. Keep me posted and allow time for me to sail if you want to reconnect on the boat. I'll be back aboard tomorrow night, but she's two day's sailing east of our old place. Let me know where to meet you; lots to catch up on.

As for my other female correspondent, I was in something of a quandary. There were other ways for us to communicate besides the satellite phone. She cautioned me against using them. That was a red flag; had she not said that, I would have already been in touch with her. Reading between the lines, I was on my own until I heard from her again.

That made me a free agent, for the moment. If something happened to her, her boss would be in touch, but I was in a strictly passive role as far as that was concerned. Her boss knew all about me, but I knew nothing about her boss. Hence my willingness to encourage Mary to count on my help.

That could all change, though, depending on who got to me first. I couldn't hazard a guess as to who would win that race, and I wasn't sure who I would prefer, either.

If Mary won and I cast my lot with her, I would probably be finished with my client. But I didn't know for sure. And at this stage, I didn't know if that was a bad thing.

Severing my ties to my client would be complex, but I wasn't unprepared. I had plenty of money stashed in obscure but accessible places, and several identities my client didn't know about. There was facial identification to worry about, but I knew my way around that pretty well. They would never dare to release my fingerprints. That could cause unimaginable problems for the government, given the places the prints might have been found.

All they could do without embarrassing themselves would

be to send somebody to kill me. Given how much I knew about their tricks, I would be a hard target; I was rumored to be their best assassin. Was I willing to risk that for Mary?

I wasn't sure of the answer to that. But I might risk it for the pure fun of it. With Mary on my team, it would be a hell of a game. But I wasn't sure how I would know if Mary was on my team.

That was my first question for her, and I didn't know how she could answer it to my satisfaction. Early on, Mary was less than honest with me.

When I rolled off the settee berth and crashed to the cabin sole, I realized that I somehow fell asleep. Before my mind engaged my problems again, I moved up to the V-berth in the forward cabin, taking a stack of the cushions from the settee with me.

I crawled into the V-berth and arranged the extra cushions to wedge me in place. I guess I fell back asleep, because the next time I opened my eyes, it was getting light outside.

17

BEFORE THE FIRST OPENING OF THE DRAWBRIDGE, I WENT ASHORE in the dinghy and took care of my inbound clearance with the Dutch authorities. Back on the boat, I ate breakfast before the first scheduled bridge opening. By the time I got through the bridge opening, the charter company was open for business.

After I finished the paperwork to turn in *Best Offer*, it was mid-morning. As soon as I stepped outside the charter office, my personal cellphone rang. Surprised, I shifted my duffle bag from my right hand, slinging it over my shoulder. I worked the phone from the pocket of my jeans and answered without taking time to check the caller ID.

"Hello?"

"Good morning, Finn. Just keep walking out the marina entrance and across the street. Go out onto Kim Sha Beach and walk along like you're looking at the boats in the anchorage. You got my voice yet?"

"Yes." *My client.*

"Good. Once I'm sure nobody's following you, I'll approach you. Don't look around for me; I'll spot you. Just play along and act surprised when I call out to you." She disconnected the call.

I did as she said. It was a short walk, although I was stuck for a couple of minutes waiting to get across Welfare Road, which crosses the drawbridge. It's a main artery on the Dutch side of the island, and the traffic was still messed up from the bridge opening half an hour ago.

Walking along the beach just above the surf line, I heard her say, "Finn! I can't believe it."

I turned to see a woman about my age approaching me. She was a little above average height, well-tanned. The orange bikini set off her skin tone with a dazzling effect. There was some gauzy-looking orange fabric knotted around her hips. A big straw hat and sunglasses hid her face.

I smiled and nodded.

"You're the last person I expected to run into here," she said. "How have you been? It's been ages since I've seen you."

Yes. Like since never. That's ages, I guess. "I'm doing all right. How have you been?"

"Great," she said. "Even better since I've run into you. Got time to catch up with an old lover?"

"Sure thing," I said.

She stepped in close for a hug and gave me a kiss on the cheek. "It's great to see you."

"You, too," I say. *Never would have guessed who this woman was. Not at all what I envisioned. She's —*

"Yeah," she said, her voice soft. "Nobody's following you. You think you're clean?"

"Yes."

"Good." She dropped the hug, snaking her right arm around my waist. "Put your left arm around me and let's stroll along the edge of the water. Act the part — two former lovers, maybe thinking about a fling for old time's sake."

As we walked, she said, "You got my text about the phone?"

"I took care of it."

"Good. I have a new one for you. And one for me, too. Both off the books."

"Okay," I said. "Off the books?"

"Yeah. You and I are both off the books, too."

"What's that mean?"

"Well, in your case, it's nothing new. You wouldn't know it, but you've been off the books ever since you retired. No record of anything about you in the active files."

"But..." I shook my head.

She laughed. Her laugh was nice, fun to hear. "Yeah. You're the ultimate deniable asset. You couldn't tell the difference, could you?"

"No. What about the passport? For the girl?"

"You're a legendary figure. People are thrilled to do you favors, even though you're not active any more. Don't over-think it. We have ways to take care of things like that. You'll always be one of us."

"Nice to know." I tried to keep my voice even, but I guess I failed.

"Just roll with it, Finn. Don't get cross."

"Okay. Sorry."

"I understand. This is probably a good time for me to tell you that you're imagining all this; none of it's really happening."

"Does that mean what I think it does?"

"Probably. This whole situation is way beyond classified. I'm not even here. In fact, I'm no longer a government employee. I've been terminated."

"I'm sorry if I caused — "

She paused and stepped around to face me, putting a finger across my lips. "Nothing for you to apologize for. It's all a matter of optics. My boss needed a scapegoat; his boss is livid over this."

"The George Kelley query?" I raised my eyebrows.

"Yes, exactly."

"Sorry you paid the price."

"Not my first time, Finn, and it won't be my last. But I'm history until we get through this. You understand what I mean?"

"Maybe. Who do I report to, if you're out of the loop?"

"You're retired, silly. You don't report to anybody."

"Really?"

"Really. But I could use your help on a purely informal basis."

"What do I call you, anyway?"

"Nora will do. Nora Thomas, if you need more. Okay?"

"Okay, Nora. You're operating on your own?"

"Yes. No government blessing for my actions. That bother you?"

"How do I know I can trust you?"

"You've trusted me for almost 20 years. I've never led you astray, have I?"

"No."

"And you're a man who sizes people up accurately, or you'd be dead by now. So I know you trust your judgment. You in?"

"I think so. There's one thing bothering me, though."

"Mary Elizabeth O'Brien," she said, smiling, a gleam in her eye.

"Yeah. What do you think about her?"

"She's a lucky woman."

"Huh? What do you — "

"If I were a man and you were a woman, I wouldn't dare say this. If I weren't your boss, I'd be giving Mary Elizabeth a run for her money. But I guess I'm safe. You can hardly report me to H.R. for making an inappropriate comment to a male subordinate when we're both unemployed."

"Ha, ha," I said. "I'm serious. I — "

"Hey, Finn! Come on. Let a girl have a little fun. I was just teasing."

"Yeah, sure. That's what they all say. Hashtag Metoo, huh?"

"All right, be that way. I'm sorry."

"I'm not offended; I was just teasing, too. But if you weren't my boss, Mary might have a problem. I pictured you as — "

"Okay, Finn. Shut up. Back to work. We've both had our fun. Maybe we can talk about the other later; we're going to have time together today. Meanwhile, tell me about Mary Elizabeth."

"I assumed you ran a check on her."

"Yeah. And we got a big fat nothing. At least nothing that she didn't put there for somebody to find."

"That's encouraging. I wondered what you'd discover if you ran her. I'm afraid I don't know much more than you do." I gave Nora a quick summary of my history with Mary, from the time I met her until she went on the run in Ste. Anne.

"Interesting," Nora said. "A hired killer, and an attractive woman to boot. I've heard of women in that game, but I always thought they were urban myths."

"She's no myth. She's flesh and bone, and a stone-cold killer."

"But here's the real question, Finn. Do you trust her?"

"Maybe. Under controlled circumstances."

"Can you elaborate?"

"If our interests are the same, I trust her."

"That's about as good as it gets in our business," Nora said.

"Yeah, but it leaves some exposure. She's out there doing her thing. And she wants me to help. I'm not sure what's driving her, so I don't know about the common interests."

"You're in touch with her, then?"

"Yes."

"How much does she know about you?"

"The usual. Retired Army, no details. But she suspects what I did in St. Vincent."

"Suspects?"

"Circumstantial. It happened while I left her alone, and she heard it on the news. The timing fit, and she knew I took the ferry to Kingstown. Plus, she saw me deal with her attackers in Puerto Real."

"You said you just helped her; she did most of the heavy work."

"That's right. But a pro can always spot another pro. It's what keeps us alive."

"Yeah, I can see that. That's okay. If you trust her, you and I could use her help."

"Like I said, I trust her as long as our interests are the same."

"I think they are. I'm not sure she knows that, but it won't take much to convince her."

"Why do you say that?"

"Now we're getting to the sticky part. If I tell you this next bit, there's no backing out, okay? Mary Elizabeth or no Mary Elizabeth. Her participation will be your call, but if you and I keep talking, you're locked in. We clear on that?"

"Yes."

"Good. Let's go up to my room. We can get a room service lunch, if you like. I've got things to give you."

18

Nora kept her arm around my waist and walked me to one of the beachfront hotels. An elevator from the beach level took us to a third-floor exterior walkway that looked out over the water.

"Act like you're about to score, Finn," she said, looking up at me with an expectant grin and squeezing my waist.

I did my best. "Somebody watching?"

"You never know. It's best to stay in character. Besides, I like the way it feels. We desk jockeys don't get to do much playacting."

"You're pretty convincing," I said.

She giggled. So much for staying in character. We stopped in front of a room. I was a little nervous when she took a key card out of her bikini top and swiped it through the door's lock.

I needn't have worried. Once the door latched behind us, she was all business. She ditched the hat and the sunglasses and unzipped a carry-on bag that was on a luggage stand. She rummaged for a second and handed me a new satellite phone.

"The unlock procedure's the same as the old one," she said.

"But the location tracking is disabled on this one. Are you going back to the BVI this afternoon?"

"I planned to. That okay?"

"Sure. But use this." She handed me a dog-eared passport in the name of John Fincastle. "Like the fort in the Bahamas."

"Any reason to think the one I've been using is compromised?"

"No. It was clean when I checked yesterday. But it never hurts to keep 'em guessing."

I nodded and put the passport in my pocket. I unzipped a hidden pocket inside my duffel bag and put my old passport in there.

She handed me an envelope. "John Fincastle's life story. I'll give you a chance to read it before you leave me."

"Okay."

"You hungry? The food here's good."

"I'm okay. You go ahead."

"I'm going to order for both of us, then," she said, reaching for the room phone. "For appearance's sake."

She ordered two mahi-mahi sandwiches with fries and four Heinekens. When she hung up the phone, she messed up the freshly made bed. "In case the waiter notices," she said.

I nodded, but kept silent.

"Okay, Finn. Have a seat." She gestured at a small round table in the corner and pulled out a chair for herself. "Ready for this?"

"Sure. You said you thought Mary Beth's interests are the same as ours?"

"Mary Beth," she said. "Okay. Not Mary Elizabeth, then. Yeah. The FBI thinks she killed a couple named Dailey in Florida a few months ago. Wealthy property developers, but they were really laundering money for a guy named Rory O'Hanlon. O'Hanlon was a kingpin in the Irish Mafia. He was also Mrs. Dailey's brother."

When she paused, I said, "That matches what I heard, too."

"From Mary Beth?"

"Sort of. She gave me bits and pieces, with some embellishment. Not about killing them, though. She claimed she used to work for them when she was in college and that she found them, dead. Butchered, she said."

"The butchered part's right," Nora said. "What else do you know?"

"What you told me is a good match for what I got from Frankie Dailey. He — "

She held up her hand. "Frankie Dailey? You said something on the phone a while back about him and bad fish, but I wasn't clear on what you meant. He's still missing."

"Yeah. He's going to stay missing." I told her more about my encounter with Frankie in Ste. Anne. "There was another guy with him, but I don't know who he was. Just muscle, not important."

"Frankie Dailey told you O'Hanlon hired Mary Beth to kill his parents? Why would O'Hanlon do that? Mrs. Dailey was his sister."

"Frankie caught them skimming and ratted them out to his uncle, according to what he told me."

"His own parents?"

"Yeah. Nice guy, huh?"

"So your girlfriend butchered them?" she asked.

"Sounds like she may have. Frankie said she was supposed to retrieve the money and a bunch of incriminating files that the Daileys had. The files were locked in a safe. My guess is that she had a little trouble convincing them to give her the combination."

She was quiet for a few seconds, thinking about that.

"The FBI says O'Hanlon and several of his minions were found dead on a yacht named *Aeolus* in Ste. Anne, Martinique. You know anything about that?" she asked.

"Maybe," I said. "Circumstantial, again, but according to Frankie, O'Hanlon's boys snatched Mary Beth off the street in Ste. Anne. Frankie came to get me; they were going to question both of us. I didn't like the sound of that, so I tied him up and left him on my boat. I went to see if Mary Beth needed help. By the time I got to *Aeolus*, the local cops were counting the bodies, trying to figure out what happened. I got a text from Mary Beth as I was leaving the scene. She was glad to see I survived my encounter with Frankie. Said she would be in touch when she could. I went back to the boat and finished dealing with Frankie and his pal."

"So you think she killed them? How many were there?"

I shrugged. "I don't know. Not enough, apparently."

"I think I like this woman," Nora said. "Sign her up."

"For what?" I asked.

"I don't know yet. You said she was supposed to retrieve some incriminating records?"

"Yeah, and money."

"The money doesn't matter. What do you know about the records?"

"They're in my laptop."

She raised her eyebrows and blinked. "What?"

"In my laptop. You got a memory card?"

She took a cheap cellphone from somewhere in that cloud of fabric around her hips and popped the back off. Using a fingernail, she extracted a microSD card and handed it to me.

I unzipped my duffle bag and retrieved the laptop. It took a couple of minutes to copy the files to her card. I pulled it out of the computer and gave it back to her.

'What's on here?" she asked.

"I think it's what got the Daileys butchered. I can't make any sense of it. Mary Beth said it requires context to extract the meaning."

"Yeah, okay. I have an idea on that. I have friends that do context. Does she have this stuff?"

"Yes. I think she's working her way through it; maybe picking up on that context."

"Uh-huh. Is she in the States?"

"That's my guess. Why?"

"O'Hanlon's associates back home are dropping like flies. The FBI thinks there's a war within the mob. You think it could be Mary Beth?"

"Yeah. She said she was tying up loose ends."

"You know who she's working for?"

"No, not for sure. But I'd say there's a good chance she's working for herself, at this point. She took maybe 15 or 20 million dollars from O'Hanlon's organization, as best I can figure."

"She double-crossed them?" Nora asked, raising her eyebrows.

"I'm not sure who double-crossed whom. She's just looking out for herself. O'Hanlon would have viewed her as a liability, even though all she did was kill the Daileys and retrieve the files, like he hired her to do. She was on her way to deliver the files to him when she was ambushed by some of his people. She got the better of them, but after that, killing O'Hanlon was a matter of self-preservation for her. The others just got in her way, probably."

"You don't know the half of it, Finn. This is about more than Mary Beth killing off a bunch of guys who deserve worse. Don't forget your pal George Kelley."

"No, I haven't forgotten. I figured you'd get to that."

"He's dirty. I don't know how high up in the FBI the corruption goes, but it goes all the way to the top in Homeland Security."

"Wait," I said. "Why Homeland Security?"

"ICE. People smuggling. Selling green cards."

"But that sounds like penny ante stuff, Nora."

"We're talking wholesale. Tens of thousands of green cards, expedited processing for citizenship. It goes way beyond O'Hanlon's bunch. Money laundering's just the tip of the iceberg. The DEA may be compromised, too."

"How high up the food chain?"

"In the DEA and ICE? The top. Maybe higher. Certainly wider."

"Jesus," I said. "You mean — "

"I don't know if it goes that high. We're still checking."

"What's going to happen?"

"Too early to say. The first step's to gather the facts."

"What do you want me to do?"

"Can you reconnect with Mary Beth?"

"Yeah, but why do you want me to do that?"

"Because she appears to be making sense of those files."

"Why do you say that?"

"There's a pattern to her actions. But it's only evident after the fact."

"I thought you said you had a way to do that, to ferret out the meaning in the material."

"We're dealing with data that only has meaning if you know the context, as you said earlier."

"Actually, it was Mary Beth who said that."

"Right. The broader our perspective, the better our deductions will be. Do you need to go back to the States to get reacquainted with her? I can arrange for somebody to take care of your boat."

"No, I don't think so. Last I heard from her, she wants to meet up down here soon and make plans. She suggested that she might be able to use my help."

Nora grinned. "Great minds, and all that."

"Yeah. I was worried about how that would play with you and your chain of command, but..."

"But now you know. Just keep me in the loop."

"That may be tough, once Mary Beth and I get started."

"Why's that?"

"There's not much privacy on a small boat."

"I thought you trusted her."

"To a point, yeah. But that doesn't mean I'll tell her about you."

"She's bound to suspect you work for somebody, Finn. Tell her, but keep my affiliation vague."

"Given what you've told me, I couldn't do anything else, even if I wanted."

"Yeah, I know. Me either, but that's my problem. You okay with this new arrangement?"

"Yeah. I'm still taking direction from you. Like you said, we have a track record. But I do have a question."

"What's that?"

"I never figured I was your one and only."

"No?" She smiled. "I didn't think you did. I would have been surprised if you were that naïve. Is that your question?"

"Sort of. It's not history that I — "

"If there were others working for me now, I wouldn't tell you. You know that."

I nodded.

"But since there aren't, I don't see any harm in it."

I raised my eyebrows. "Just you and me, huh?"

"And Mary Beth, if she agrees."

"A threesome."

She smiled. "Don't do that, Finn. I know I started it; I'm sorry about my remark earlier. It was unprofessional."

"Forgotten, then," I said. "But it's nice to put a person with that disembodied voice I've been hearing all these years."

"Yeah, I agree."

"But you already knew everything about me."

"Not everything. That's why I came down here. I had

pictures and descriptions, but you were two-dimensional. Like you said, it's nice to match a real person with all that data."

I held her eyes for several long seconds.

"You need to catch a plane," she said. "We'll meet again. I like you. And maybe you can introduce me to Mary Beth."

19

My flight from St. Martin arrived at Tortola's Terrance
B. Lettsome International Airport at 3:40 pm. By the time I got
through customs and immigration and made my way to Soper's
Hole, it was almost time for an early dinner.

Tired from the last couple of days, I planned to drop my
duffle bag on *Island Girl* and go to one of the overpriced restaurants in the marina. The next morning, I could settle my bill for
dockage and go back to the nice, quiet anchorage off Fort
Recovery. That would be a good place to kick back for a few
days while I worked out the details of meeting up with Mary
Beth.

Alas, it wasn't to be. As soon as I stepped into *Island Girl's*
cockpit, I saw the splintered teak where somebody pried out
the hasp and staple that secured the companionway hatch. The
locked padlock was still hanging there, useless.

At least, the bastard who broke in closed the hatch to keep
out the rain from the afternoon showers. Looking down into
the cockpit footwell, I could see that the two cockpit lockers
received the same treatment as the companionway hatch. So
much for the marina's security guards.

A quick look in the cockpit lockers satisfied me that nothing was missing. But there wasn't much there to tempt a thief, anyway. I slid the companionway hatch forward and took out the drop boards, stacking them in the cockpit.

The area below deck was a mess. Everything from the lockers was scattered on the cabin sole. I shoved aside the stuff on the chart table, making a big enough space to put my bag down.

Starting at the foot of the companionway ladder, I picked up whatever was immediately underfoot and returned it to its normal place. Most of the stuff back there went in the galley lockers.

Thankfully, none of the glass jars that held gooey things like jelly and condiments was broken. The dishes were plastic, so they were intact as well. In ten minutes, I put the galley back in order.

The charts, books, and papers from the navigation area weren't too hard to deal with. Soon, I was in the main saloon. Towels, bedding, and odds and ends of clothing were scattered there.

The locker that held Mary Beth's stuff was at the forward end of the saloon on the starboard side. Her belongings received special attention. The intruder emptied her backpack — up-ended it and shook it, from the looks of things.

The clothing she bought in Ste. Anne wasn't spared. Seams where anything might have been hidden were ripped out. I made a quick check of the backpack itself. Feeling the seam where the microSD card was hidden, I smiled. It was still there. It must have been small enough to escape the burglar's notice.

I stepped over Mary's things and took a quick look in the head and the fore-cabin. Both appeared to have been given only a cursory going-over. Based on the attention Mary's belongings received, I suspected that this was not the work of an ordinary thief.

George Kelley was probably responsible. The coast guard search had spotted Mary Beth's things, and somebody returned for an in-depth look. But they missed the only thing that could have been of interest to them. I chuckled at their folly as I put the rest of the things away. The mess could have been worse.

On my way up the companionway ladder, I picked up my duffle bag. I stepped out into the cockpit and put the drop boards in, closing the hatch. Climbing over the lifelines, I walked up the dock and ambled along restaurant row.

Settling on a place that advertised fresh ahi tuna steaks cooked to order, I got a table. The waitress wasted no time; she took my order as I sat down. In a couple of minutes, she brought me a beer. Seeing my laptop, she fumbled a card with the WiFi password from the pocket of her apron.

Handing me the card, she gave me a warm smile and said, "Food soon come. Jus' wave if you need anyt'ing."

I thanked her and powered up the laptop, checking the blind email drop in hopes of word from Mary Beth. I wasn't disappointed.

Guessing you'll be back on the boat tonight. Meet the 2:30 Miami flight at St. Thomas tomorrow. Don't reply. Already on my way. See you soon, sailor.

As I was putting away the laptop, the waitress brought my food. "Anyt'ing else right now?"

"No, thanks." As I ate, I considered my options for meeting Mary Beth. Taking the boat to St. Thomas put me back in U.S. waters, in Special Agent Kelley's jurisdiction. If his minions were behind the search of *Island Girl,* he probably wasn't interested in the boat any longer. But he might be curious about what I was up to. I didn't want to lead him to Mary Beth.

Frankie's tracking device was on the boat, still. I could remove it, or even plant it on another boat, if I wanted to confuse Kelley. But odds were high that someone was watching the boat, anyway. That meant they would try to follow me when I went to the airport, no matter what I did with the boat.

Not knowing Mary Beth's plans, I decided to leave *Island Girl* in the marina. There were several storefront operations that offered diving and snorkeling excursions here. In the morning, I would sign up for one. If someone were watching me, they wouldn't follow an excursion boat to a dive site.

They would wait here for me to come back. When the excursion boat returned without me after a few hours, the watchers would be stumped.

I finished my dinner and went for a stroll along the waterfront, checking out the dive and snorkel operations. I narrowed the options to three, each of which used sizable boats.

I wanted to be part of a crowd when I left in the morning. That way, when the excursion boat came back without me, the watcher might think I slipped ashore in the group without being noticed. By the time they realized I was missing, Mary Beth and I could be somewhere else.

20

THE VIRGIN ISLANDS ARE OVERRUN BY AMERICAN TOURISTS. That's a blessing and a curse. That next morning, it was a blessing, at least for me. American tourists are an unkempt bunch, so it wasn't hard for me to disguise myself.

I wore flip-flops and a pair of baggy, quick-drying nylon shorts that doubled as swim trunks. My T-shirt came from one of those beachfront places that sell them three for $10. It advertised a product I never heard of. A mildly obscene baseball cap and mirrored sunglasses completed my outfit.

My oversized fanny pack was waterproof, and it held my wallet and the passport Nora gave me. The special satellite phone plus another tourist T-shirt and a floppy canvas sun hat were in there, too. And my Smartphone, of course.

I carried my snorkeling gear in a mesh bag. The fee for the trip included the use of gear from the excursion company, but I told them I preferred to use my own.

"Lotta people do, mon," the lady in the booth told me. "Don' like them snorkel ever'body put they mout' on. Mm-hmm."

I didn't bother to explain that my reason was different. I didn't want to steal their stuff; that would make me more memorable. What I was planning would be unusual enough without adding petty theft.

The other ten people on the snorkeling trip were dressed just like me. I couldn't tell myself apart from the other males when I caught our reflection in a plate-glass window as we were lining up to board the excursion boat.

Fifteen minutes after we boarded, we finished a scenic run around Frenchman's Cay. The skipper picked up a mooring near the reefs that lined the north shore of the big cove just east of the Cay. We were only a half mile from the marina we departed from, but the tourists didn't realize that.

While the mate passed out gear to everyone, I told the skipper I would bail out here after I got a look at the reef. He looked surprised, but I slipped him a $20 bill and he nodded.

"I'm just anchored over there in Soper's Hole," I said, pointing across the little isthmus that connected Frenchman's Cay to the mainland of Tortola.

"Ah," he said, pocketing the bill.

If he thought that was odd, he kept it to himself, turning his attention to one of two young women in skimpy bikinis. They were having trouble figuring out how to adjust their buoyancy compensator vests.

I couldn't have asked for a better distraction. The skipper was absorbed in the project, tugging the stiff fabric of the inflatable vest to fit over her ample bosom, smoothing out the wrinkles while she giggled.

The mate was having the same trouble with her friend's vest. The four of them were laughing and flirting while I put on my gear. I clipped the lanyard of my almost empty mesh bag to the belt of my fanny pack. There was nothing in the mesh bag but my flip-flops.

The mate and the skipper didn't even notice as I slipped over the side. Thanks to the two bikini girls, they wouldn't miss me when I didn't return.

I swam along at the back of the pack as my fellow tourists paddled toward the reef, letting them get ahead of me. Once I was several yards behind the crowd, I turned and swam east along the shore for a few hundred yards. Treading water, I pushed my mask up on my forehead and looked around. Nobody was watching me.

Working my way into knee-deep water, I took off my gear, putting it back in the mesh bag. Once ashore, I unzipped my fanny pack and took out a quick-drying microfiber towel. Soon, I was attired in a dry T-shirt, a floppy sun hat, and a different pair of sunglasses from the ones I wore when I boarded the boat.

Picking my way over the rocky shore in my flip-flops, I made my way to the road that runs around the perimeter of the island. In a few minutes, I flagged down a bus that was headed east. After swinging through several little communities, the bus dropped me in Road Town. From there, I boarded a passenger ferry to Red Hook, St. Thomas.

An hour later, I walked down the gangway and showed my passport to the U.S. immigration officer at the terminal.

"Welcome back to the U.S., Mr. Fincastle."

"Thanks," I said.

Outside the gate, I caught a dollar taxi to the airport. My roundabout route took me almost three hours, but I was sure no one followed me.

The excursion boat I boarded in Soper's Hole would be dropping off its passengers now. Thinking about the reaction of the person who might be watching for me there brought a smile to my face.

I found a video display listing arriving flights; Mary Beth's flight was on time. With over two hours to kill, I went in search of a restaurant. Once I ordered my food, I took my cellphone and the satellite phone out of my fanny pack. The phones were in a heavyweight waterproof bag in case the fanny pack leaked.

While I waited for my lunch, I checked for messages. Nobody was trying to reach me. I didn't expect to hear from Mary Beth, but I wouldn't have been surprised to find a text from Nora.

Almost 24 hours had passed since I left her at the hotel in St. Martin. I wondered where she was. Oddly, I missed her and was more than a little worried about her. I chuckled to myself and took a sip of beer. In all the years I took orders from her, I never thought much about her until now.

Meeting her face to face after all this time made me curious about her. What kind of life did she have? She seemed like a normal woman, personable, attractive. Now that I was safely out of her presence, I admitted that she was sexy, even. And she knew it.

She flirted with me, and she was annoyed with herself for doing it. For a few seconds, there, we were like two regular people.

But we weren't. Not by any definition of regular. We both lived in dark places, the recesses of society that most people didn't know about.

She surprised me when she told me to enlist Mary Beth, but in hindsight, that wasn't so strange. The three of us shared some uncommon traits.

I recognized a kindred spirit in Mary Beth right away, but Nora, or whatever her real name was... Well, she was nothing more than a bureaucratic voice on the phone until yesterday.

People like me and Mary Beth, we looked at other people the way predators looked at prey. Oh, sure, there were a few others out there who were more like us, but they were rare. And most of them were unbalanced, too self-absorbed to be much danger to people like us.

Nora wasn't like that. She was neither predator nor prey, at least not the way I classified people. She was something else. Maybe something even scarier than Mary Beth and me.

Nora hinted that I was her only asset at the moment, but I knew she ran teams of agents like me in the past. Most of the lives I took in the last 20 years, I took at her command. I always pictured her sitting in an office somewhere with no idea of what havoc she wreaked on the people we called targets.

Now I knew what she looked like, what it felt like to put my arms around her. That woman was responsible for more deaths than Mary Beth and I were together, most likely. But she was a warm, friendly person. In a different world, I could imagine the two of us —

"Sir?"

I jumped when I realized there was a hand on my shoulder. I blinked and saw that my food was on the table in front of me. Looking up, I could tell the waitress was worried. I forced a smile.

"Sorry. I drifted off."

She nodded and gave my shoulder a little squeeze before she dropped her hand. "I thought maybe somethin' done happen bad when you don' answer me the firs' time I ask can I get you anyt'ing else. You all right, mon?"

"Fine, thanks." *But I wasn't. I was rattled to my core. If I'm awake, I'm aware of everything around me. Except just now, this woman put a plate in front of me and touched me, and I was oblivious. She could have...*

"You looked like you was somewhere far away. But mon, you was happy, wherever you was. Almos', I hate to disturb, but I was 'fraid the fish curry get cold. Sorry if I startle you, mon."

"It's okay. Thanks; cold fish curry's no good."

"You need anyt'ing else, you jus' let me know. Enjoy the lunch."

"All right. Thanks."

21

I watched as the last few people from the Miami flight entered the arrivals area. There was no sign of Mary Beth. After a thirty-second lull in the stream of passengers, the flight crew came out, and then I knew for sure she wasn't on the flight.

"Psst. Don't turn around, Finn. Five minutes, in the bar closest to the restrooms."

She was behind me; I recognized her voice. I gave her a few seconds to get clear. Shrugging, I put a frown on my face and walked to the nearest bank of video monitors.

I waited as the display scrolled through the originating cities, watching for Miami flights. Taking out my cellphone, I pretended to check my voicemail, and then I shook my head. I glanced up at the clock above the video monitors and shrugged again, turning and walking toward the bar.

There were quite a few people sitting among piles of luggage. I found an open table and tossed my mesh bag of snorkel gear on it, marking it as occupied. Mary Beth wasn't there yet, so I went over to the bar and bought two beers.

When I turned back to the table, there was a grungy girl with stringy green hair sitting there with her back to me.

Wearing a halter top and greasy jeans, she rummaged in a bulging cloth shopping bag on her lap.

Annoyed, I went to the table and put the beers down while I picked up my mesh bag and hooked it to my belt, ready to look for another table. The girl looked up from the bag in her lap. My eyes were drawn to the hardware dangling from her nose ring.

"Hey, sailor. What's the matter? Don't want to buy a girl a drink?"

Stunned, I did my best to hide my surprise. I dropped the mesh bag on the floor by the table. As I settled into my chair, she fiddled with the nose jewelry and unhooked most of it, leaving a simple gold ring there.

"Gets in the way of drinking from a glass," she said. "It's really good to see you. Sorry for the drama, but I wanted to make sure you weren't followed."

"Me, too. I'm surprised you recognized me with the hat and sunglasses."

"Well, it helped that you were the only one left in the greeting area after the people got off the flight."

"I didn't see you come through the gate," I said. "The hair would have caught my attention."

"No. I wasn't on that flight. I got here earlier. You like my hair?"

"I could get used to it, I guess. There's more to your appeal than your appearance."

"Aw, that's sweet. But don't bother."

"Don't bother?"

She laughed. "You look so disappointed. I only meant don't bother getting used to the hair. It's temporary."

"Good. A darker green would suit you better."

"Same old smart-ass. I've missed you."

"Really? I hear you've been busy."

She frowned. "Where'd you hear that?"

"Long story," I said. "How long do you think we should sit here?"

"You have somewhere to go?"

"No. Not right off. I don't think the boat's a good idea, though."

"I wondered about that. We should probably cut this short, just in case."

She rummaged in her bag again, setting several things on the table. Then she shifted the bag to the table top, knocking some items to the floor. "Be a gentleman and pick those up. Palm the crumpled piece of paper."

I bent to retrieve her junk, and when I sat up, she held the bag in her lap again. She reached across the table and took the stuff I was holding.

"Thanks," she said, dropping it in the bag. "Give me a 15-minute head-start."

She took a last swig of beer and stood up, slinging the bag over her shoulder as she turned and walked out of the bar. I nursed my beer, resisting the urge to look at the paper. When 15 minutes passed, I retrieved my mesh bag and stood up.

Outside the terminal, I smoothed the piece of paper. *Fiddler's Green guest house — room 213.* I walked over to the end of the taxi line. After a couple of minutes, I reached the front of the line and the dispatcher asked where I was going.

"Fiddler's Green guest house."

He shook his head. "You got an address?"

"No. Sorry. I'm supposed to meet somebody there."

Nodding, he raised a cellphone to his ear. He chattered away in heavy patois for a minute, then turned to me. "They checkin'. Gon' call me back."

He moved to the people behind me. Soon, I was the last person waiting.

"They don' call back," he said. "Sorry, mon. I try again."

He used the phone again. This time the conversation didn't last long.

"They don' call because they t'ink I am joking. You sure 'bout the Fiddler's Green, mon?"

"Yes. Why?"

"They say it's not in the bes' neighborhood. Surprised a white mon want to go there. But I got the address, if you sure."

"I'm sure."

He nodded and waved for the next cab to pull up. As I got in, he leaned into the window and gave the driver an address. The driver looked at me, then back at the dispatcher, who nodded. The driver shrugged and returned the nod. We pulled away into traffic.

Ten minutes later, the taxi stopped in front of a two-story concrete-block building that looked more like a factory than a hotel. A faded, hand-lettered sign in the only window on the ground floor marked it as the Fiddler's Green. The window was protected by sturdy burglar bars.

"You sure 'bout this, mon?" the driver asked.

"Yes."

"Ten dollars, then. You want me to wait? No way you gonna get another taxi to come pick you up if you change your mind."

"Bad neighborhood?" I asked.

He shrugged. "Jus' the people here, they don' use taxis. Cos' too much. So we don' come here. Mebbe somebody call taxi to come here an' the driver t'ink he gon' get robbed, see."

"I see. I'll be fine, but thanks for offering." I paid him and got out, watching as he drove away.

The guest house entrance was a steel fire door, and it was locked. I pressed the buzzer and saw a flicker of movement through the eye-level peephole. I heard the lock release, and the door opened. The man inside looked me over for a few seconds. He was big and looked solid, like he could handle himself. The scars on his face and arms told me he survived a few knife fights.

"Twenty dollars," he said. "For up to 24 hours. In advance. Room 120. Key's in the door."

"I'm visiting somebody."

He shrugged. "Still twenty dollars."

"Just to visit?"

"I done heard that story, mon. Twenty dollars, or get outta here."

I gave him a twenty, and he stepped back to let me in. Then he closed and re-locked the door. "You know what room?" he asked.

I nodded. "Upstairs."

"Stairs at the end of the hall," he said, as he went into a room and closed the door. I walked down the hall to the stairwell, which smelled of things I didn't want to think about. There were dead roaches, cigarette butts, and a few crushed hypodermic syringes. I held my breath and climbed the stairs.

Room 213 was about halfway down the dimly lit hall. I knocked, and the door swung open. What I could see of the room was empty; whoever opened the door was standing behind it.

"Step into the room and take your chances," Mary Beth's whisper came from behind the door. "If you're not who I'm expecting, kiss your ass goodbye, because I'll kill you in a heartbeat."

That brought a smile to my face. I stepped inside and the door closed, revealing Mary Beth, green hair and all, a folding combat knife open in her hand.

"Why'd you open the door if you didn't know who was there?"

"I was bored. I figured it might be a diversion." She closed the knife and stuck it in the pocket of her jeans.

After she latched the door, she put her arms around my neck and gave me a lingering kiss.

"Thanks for coming," she said, still holding on.

"I'm glad to see you again." I noticed the nose ring was gone. "Nice place you've got here. Cost me $20 just to visit."

"Yeah, well, it's that kind of place, you know? But it's fairly safe in the daytime. Everybody's either unconscious or out hustling. Nighttime's a different story."

"I guess," I said, looking around the closet-sized room. It held a single bed that looked like it was World War II surplus. That was it. There were hooks on the wall for clothes and a tiny sink in the corner. "No windows. Only one way in and out. You could get trapped in here."

"They have to come through the door one at a time. That's all the edge I need."

"That's my lady. You made quick work of O'Hanlon and his friends in Ste. Anne. I came to help, but you'd left already."

"I hear Frankie's still missing."

"I'm not surprised. We won't see him again, but before he left, he told me all about you."

She laughed. "Yeah? That bastard. I hate men who kiss and tell."

22

"KISS AND TELL? YOU AND FRANKIE DAILEY WERE — "

Mary Beth laughed again. "Relax, Finn. It's just a figure of speech. Frankie wasn't my type. What exactly did he tell you?"

"He had a different slant on your relationship with the Daileys."

She grinned and pushed the green hair back from her forehead. "I'll just bet he did."

Taking a step back from me, she sat on the edge of the bed. Patting the spot beside her, she said, "Pull up a chair and tell me what he said."

I sat down next to her and nodded. "The short version is that Frankie caught his parents skimming and ratted them out to O'Hanlon. O'Hanlon hired you to kill them and retrieve their files and the money they stole. Frankie said you tried to put the screws to O'Hanlon. Kept the money and were trying to use the files for blackmail."

"That's close enough, I guess. Considering it came from Frankie, anyway. Except after I took care of the Daileys, O'Hanlon set up a meeting with me. I was supposed to hand off the money and the files, and he was going to settle up with me once he got to look everything over. That was the deal I was signed up to, but they changed the plans."

"Who changed the plans?"

"O'Hanlon, I think. Could have been Frankie, but I don't think he had that much gumption."

I frowned. "Gumption?"

"Frankie could have been planning to take what I found and go into business for himself — cut O'Hanlon out. He was greedy enough, but maybe not that smart. Either way, to me it looked like a double-cross when their goons ambushed me before the meeting. That's when I decided to cut and run."

"I see," I said. "What have you been doing since Ste. Anne?"

"You said you heard I've been busy. Where did you pick that up?"

What do I tell her? It's decision time. Nora wants me to do this, and she knows about Mary Beth. Maybe as much or more than I do. I love this woman. I want to come clean with her, and for her to come clean with me. Still, trusting outsiders can get me killed. And everybody but me is an outsider. Go for it. What the hell? If I'm wrong about her, it'll be fatal for one of us. But our odds aren't looking so good anyway.

"From my client, the person who picks my targets."

"Your targets. So, I was right about you." She locked eyes with me and held my gaze, demanding my concurrence.

"Maybe. I'm not sure what you think you know about me."

"Those people in St. Vincent? You killed them, didn't you?"

"Yes."

"On orders from the government?"

"Yes, I think so."

"You think so?"

"That's as good as it gets for me, Mary Beth. It's fuzzy; I trust the person who gives me my targets. If I have a problem with the choice, in theory I can turn it down, just like you can."

"In theory? Do you ever turn them down?"

"Not yet. I've never killed anybody who didn't deserve to die, by my reckoning. I'm not sure what would happen if I were to refuse an assignment."

"You've been doing this for 20 years?"

"Yes, give or take."

"Wow!" she said. Swallowing hard, still looking me in the eye. "I can't believe you're telling me this. You trust me? After all the lies I've told you?"

"It's not easy, but I'm trying."

"Finn, I don't scare easily, but you're frightening me. What happens if I'm not... If I don't measure up to your expectations?"

"One of us will die, for sure. You know that. I'm not sure if it'll be me or you, but only one of us will survive a betrayal."

"Why?"

"Why what?"

"Why did you decide to trust me, at this point?"

"Life's a gamble. I figure my odds of surviving are better if I work with you. That means I have to trust you."

"Your odds of surviving?"

"Yes. I think both of us have a better chance of getting through the next few months alive if we're working together. You already said you needed my help. Now I'm telling you I need yours."

"You? Or the government?"

"Me. I'm not sure about my relationship with the government now. Things have changed in the last few days."

"Are you freelancing?"

"I may be. I don't know. I've still got my old contact. She may be able to give us some help. It's an unclear situation. Even more unclear than usual. I can give you more details later, but they're not going to be of much use to you. My contact wants us to work together."

"Us? Like, you and me?"

"Yes. You and me."

"To do what?"

"To follow up on whatever leads we find in those files of yours."

"Your contact knows about the files?"

"Yes. And maybe she can help with some intelligence. I gave her the files."

"She? You work for a woman?"

"She's been my contact for a long time. There are other people I talk to sometimes, but they're just for technical support. Like the guy I called for your passport that time. To say I work for her? Not sure that was ever accurate. But it's definitely not accurate now. Like I said, she's been cut loose. Think of her more like a silent partner, for now. She's got informal access to information that might be useful, and she wants to help us finish what you've started."

"What's her motivation?"

"Good question. I've never known. She's been my contact for a long time. Her track record with me is good."

"Did you tell her about me?"

"No. She knew already. Maybe from the passport, maybe some other way. She's okay with our relationship, with us working together."

"Will I meet this woman?"

"I don't know. I just met her for the first time two days ago."

"But you said she's given you targets for 20 years."

"That's right. I still don't know her real name. And I'm not sure I'd recognize her if I saw her again. That's part of the way the government can get away with denying that people like me exist."

"Is she going to put any constraints on us?"

"That's up to us. We make the final decisions. She's there for guidance and support, not to give us orders. And if we do something she doesn't like, there won't be any way to tie it back to her. That's the way it's always worked; it hasn't changed."

"How can I say no? Sounds like a perfect setup. And I get to hang out with a hot guy on a boat, in the bargain."

"Yeah. Speaking of that, we need to figure out what to do about the boat. There's that tracking device that Frankie's bunch planted in Bequia. I'm 99 percent sure that Kelley knows about it."

"Kelley?" Mary Beth interrupted.

"The crooked FBI agent in St. Thomas. I mentioned him in one of my emails."

"Oh, right. But not by name."

"Special Agent George Kelley. They're bound to be watching the boat. Sometime while I was gone, somebody broke in and went through your stuff. But they didn't find the microSD card."

"You think Kelley's behind that?"

"Yes. He tipped his hand when he rattled off our itinerary after we left Bequia. The only way he could have known was if he had access to the tracker, or Frankie told him."

"So that's why you think he's crooked?"

"Partly. There's more, but I've got a question for you first."

"Okay. Ask."

"Kelley said Frankie was a confidential informant. You believe that?"

"No. But if he was, then Kelley might be straight. Is that what you're getting at?"

"Well, I thought that might be a possibility, but not any more."

"I've been mistaken before, Finn."

"Maybe, but there's more. My contact — let's call her Nora. She used that name in St. Martin. It's the only name I've heard for her."

"So you met *Nora* in St. Martin. You said you were away

from the boat for two days. Were you with her that whole time?"

"No. I accepted a job I thought would be in St. Barth. I flew from here to St. Martin and chartered a boat. Left *Island Girl* in the BVI to keep Kelley from tracking me. I ended up sailing to Antigua to finish the job. When I returned the charter boat in St. Martin, Nora surprised me by showing up there. I told you, I never met her before."

"She pretty?" Mary Beth asked.

"Don't, Mary Beth. She's attractive, but she's not my type. Like you said about Frankie."

"Touché. I'm just teasing you, Finn."

"Okay. I'm feeling sensitive; I don't have a lot of experience with this he-she stuff. There's a generation between you and me. I don't want to mess up with you."

"Sorry. Why did Nora meet you in St. Martin?"

"To tell me that after she made an inquiry about Kelley for me, her boss's boss got his ass chewed. Nora got suspended, or maybe fired. She was vague about that. But she confirmed that Kelley is working with what's left of the O'Hanlon crowd."

"She stumbled over a trip wire, huh?"

"Big time. There's only one person in the chain of command higher than her boss's boss."

"Jesus, Finn. Are you telling me — "

"Don't even say it out loud. But yes. So the fix is in that high up."

"Does that mean the person we're not mentioning is part of this?"

"Maybe, but not necessarily. It could be that someone conned him into quashing the request without telling him why. These are politicians, remember?"

"Yeah, but..." Mary sat there, frowning and shaking her head.

"Enough about that for now. We need to figure out what to

do about the tracker on *Island Girl*. We can't use her if they're tracking her and keeping her under surveillance."

"Okay, but there are two things that come before that. I hate this place. We need to get out of here. If we can't use the boat, let's find somewhere else."

"All right. That's one thing. What's the other?"

"I've missed you," she said, swinging her legs over mine and wrapping her arms around my neck. "I've got the room for another couple of hours. May as well use it. Seize the moment, as the saying goes. Who knows when we'll get another chance?"

23

MARY BETH AND I WERE STAYING IN A TOURIST HOTEL IN CANE Garden Bay. It wasn't fancy, but it was a lot nicer than the Fiddler's Green in St. Thomas. I didn't want to leave her there, but I figured I should put in an appearance at *Island Girl* for the benefit of Kelley's surveillance team. Since Kelley was looking for Mary, we figured it would be best if I went alone.

The snorkel excursion boat I left on earlier in the day returned to Soper's Hole over an hour ago. The poster at the boat's ticket booth advertised two shore-side stops — one for lunch, and another for sundowners at a beach bar near Nanny Cay. The poster said the trip back from Nanny Cay was optional, and I didn't pay for that, just in case somebody was asking questions about me.

It was early evening when I ambled down the dock in Soper's Hole, pretending to be a little drunk. My bag of snorkel gear was slung over my shoulder, so if Kelley's people were watching, they'd figure I stayed behind at the beach bar in Nanny Cay for dinner. That assumed they noticed I didn't come back with the snorkel boat. I might have been giving them more credit than they deserved.

Island Girl was as I left her. I didn't fix the broken lock, but nobody went aboard in my absence. I left a piece of thread on the companionway sliding hatch cover's track. It was undisturbed.

I was anxious about my laptop computer. Reluctantly, I left it aboard when I went snorkeling. I didn't want to snorkel with a dry bag big enough to hold the computer; that would have been too noticeable. The computer's hard drive was encrypted, but there was stuff on it that wouldn't be easy to replace. I left it under the cushions in the V-berth — not a great hiding place, but better than the drawer at the chart table where I usually kept it. It was a relief to find it nestled under those cushions.

There was nothing else aboard that I would miss, except my stash of passports and cash. Those were in a steel box on top of the ballast casting in the keel. The box and the laptop were the reasons I came back.

The box was concealed under a half-inch-thick layer of fiberglass in the bilge. No one would find it if they didn't know it was there. Access required using a power saw to cut the bottom out of the bilge sump.

That made too much noise for me to do it in the marina. I planned to spend the night aboard and sail around to the anchorage off Fort Recovery in the morning. There was plenty of privacy there.

I would retrieve what I needed from the stash and repair the fiberglass. Once I finished, I would bring *Island Girl* back here and arrange for the marina to keep an eye on her. I would tell them I was going to be away on business for an indefinite period.

Once *Island Girl* was tucked in, I would use the dollar buses to work my way to Cane Garden Bay and Mary. I would make two trips to avoid carrying too much luggage. I didn't want to tip Kelley's people off that I was leaving.

They would figure it out eventually, but I wanted as much

of a head-start as I could get. I expected to be settled in our room at Cane Garden Bay the next evening in time for dinner with Mary.

After Mary and I renewed our acquaintance earlier this afternoon, she spent a few minutes rinsing the green dye from her hair. I watched as she became an auburn-haired beauty. She looked good, but I still liked her normal, honey-blonde look best. At least, her hair was honey blond when I met her. Who knew, for sure?

She tied a scarf around her still-damp hair before we left the Fiddler's Green in case we passed anybody who was expecting her to have the green locks. The scarf was almost the same shade of green as her former dye job.

"I'll take the scarf off when we're on the ferry," she said. "Then I'll look normal when we pass through customs and immigration."

We left the Fiddler's Green and took a ferry from Red Hook, St. Thomas, to Road Harbour, Tortola. Given that we were disguised and using passports that Kelley didn't know about, we made the trip together. In Cane Garden Bay, we checked into the hotel as Mr. and Mrs. John Fincastle. If the clerk noticed that Mary's passport was in the name of Mary Margaret Jordan, she didn't comment on it. I guess married couples with different last names were common enough nowadays.

Mary cautioned me while we were en route to Tortola that she was traveling with a new name. I was training myself to think of her as just plain Mary. When I asked where she got the passport, she told me that when she first started her current line of work, she spent several months creating false identities.

"It was such a pain in the neck I figured I might as well do several at the same time," she said. "It didn't take any longer to do them all than it would have taken to do one."

I should have guessed. She was Mary Elizabeth O'Brien when we first met. That identity fell by the wayside in Bequia, when Frankie Dailey's minions trailed us there and tried to kidnap her. We escaped, and I arranged a new identity for her on the fly. Her Mary Elizabeth O'Brien passport was in my stash in the bilge.

At the time, she marveled at how quickly I got the new passport. She was worried that it was a forgery, because she spent months becoming Mary Elizabeth O'Brien. Building an identity from scratch that was solid enough to get a real U.S. passport wasn't trivial.

I knew ways to shorten the process, though, and I assured her that her new passport was real. She became Mary Helen Maloney then, with bank accounts and credit cards to match.

That was when she started to suspect I was connected to the government. It didn't occur to me then that she established more than one solid false identity on her own. But I didn't know as much about her then.

As I got to know her better, the subject didn't come up. We were too busy with other things. After she confessed earlier this afternoon to having an assortment of passports, I asked where she kept them.

"I always have one extra with me," she said. "In case I get in a bind, like when I went on the run from Ste. Anne. But the rest are stashed in lockboxes in major East Coast cities."

What a girl; she was just my type.

We checked into the hotel and went out for a nice meal at the best restaurant in Cane Garden Bay. After dinner, I walked her back to the hotel and kissed her goodnight.

We spent several hours together from the time we met at the airport until our goodnight kiss. During our afternoon and evening together, we discussed what to do about *Island Girl* and her tracking device. I suggested finding and removing it.

"What would we do with it?" she asked.

"I could break it."

"But then they'll know you found it," Mary said. "Or at least suspect you did."

"I could put it on another boat and let some unsuspecting people lead them on a wild goose chase."

She smiled. "Fun thought. But if you're right and they have somebody watching *Island Girl*, that won't do us much good."

"We could stay in hotels," I said.

"The nice thing about a boat is the flexibility it gives us. You chartered that one in St. Martin. There must be thousands of charter boats here. I read on the plane that the BVI is the charter capital of North America. Plus, they all look alike."

"There is that," I said. "But the charter companies have all kinds of funny rules. Some of them don't want you taking their boats to certain places, or sailing at night. Besides, there's a paper trail, and they're geared up for charters that last a week or two. If we keep the boat much longer than that, it'll attract notice."

"Then let's buy one," Mary said.

We kicked that around and decided that while I retrieved what we needed from *Island Girl* tomorrow, Mary would shop for a boat. The charter companies sold them, usually after they were five years old. That seemed like a great option to both of us.

A used charter boat looked exactly like the ones still in the charter fleets. They were made up of generic, white fiberglass boats with blue canvas trim, with no distinguishing features.

Mary would start with the charter operations here in Tortola. Perhaps we could buy a boat and keep it registered in the BVI or the U.K. That would provide a little more insulation if Kelley and company came looking.

The thought of Kelley brought Nora's plight to mind. It was my query about Kelley that got her in trouble. Mary asked me earlier about Nora's incentive to keep going on her own. That was a fair question.

My first reaction was based on Nora's comment that her suspension was for appearances' sake, covering her boss's ass. Mary seemed to accept my comment about Nora's track record with me. Once I was alone with my thoughts, I wondered what Nora was up to. There was a disconnect in her story.

My role with Nora was eliminating people who were threats to our country. We didn't do investigations; we assassinated people. So what was Nora's agenda these days?

Did she have a mandate to eliminate the people who were implicated in O'Hanlon's criminal enterprise? I doubted that. But if so, where did the authority come from? It was contrary to our whole system of jurisprudence.

At my core, I'm a soldier. When I was commissioned as an officer in the Army, I took an oath to uphold the constitution. I killed many people, but I never betrayed that oath.

When I accepted a target, I knew I was acting within the scope of the government's authority in defense of my country. I made a few exceptions, but only when exercising my innate right to defend myself.

When Nora told me about her boss's boss getting chewed out over Nora's questions about Kelley, I got queasy. Unless I was missing something, that meant the president — or one of his close confidants — was protecting Kelley.

Kelley was a crook; I didn't have much doubt about that. That didn't mean I thought he should be executed without due process. Our system of laws was meant to deal with situations like Kelley's, and the process didn't involve people like me and Nora.

The president might be crooked too, or he might have been duped by one of his trusted advisors. That didn't make them targets for assassination. Again, there were established, constitutionally mandated ways to deal with that kind of situation.

So what am I into, here? And how do I square my beliefs with what Mary does? I know I'm in love, and that's irrational to begin with. Still, Mary's not an evil person.

She's not operating in a gray area; she only kills people who would kill her without blinking an eye. Same as me. It's like my innate right to defend myself, except sometimes she strikes preemptively.

Now that I think about it, all my targets have been cold-blooded killers, and beyond the reach of normal jurisprudence. Most times, I didn't give them a chance to kill me, but if I made one little mistake, they would have. Every one of them. Not much different from Mary.

Okay, Finn, maybe all that's a little bit gray. A very little bit, though. Mary's living in a world where a different set of rules applies — maybe. I need to talk with her about that, find out where she draws the line. My gut says it's somewhere I can live with, but what if it's not? Don't try to deal with everything now. One step at a time.

Mary was one thing. Nora, though, was a different kind of animal. Mary and I were both living in a kill-or-be-killed environment. As best I knew, Nora was never even close to that.

She was a link in the chain of command, passing orders to me from a duly constituted authority. In the past, there were plenty of ways for me to be sure of that. I wondered if she was still a "link in the chain of command."

How can I know? Do I stop trusting her because she was honest enough to tell me the chain of command is broken? That's not right. But I'm not willing to accept her as the sole person making decisions about who gets to live and who has to die. She doesn't have that authority any more than I do. So how's this going to work?

I would have plenty of time to think about those problems the next day, while I was working on *Island Girl*. I was exhausted from a long, exciting day. I fell asleep as soon as I closed my eyes.

24

THE NEXT EVENING, MARY TOLD ME HOW SHE SPENT HER TIME while I was working on *Island Girl* earlier. We were waiting for our dinner in another upscale restaurant in Cane Garden Bay.

"I saw two decent boats for sale at one of the charter companies," she said. "Want to look them over tomorrow?"

"Sure," I said.

"And we can just keep the registration 'as is,' at least for a while," she said. "They're anxious to sell both boats. There's language they said they could put in the contract that would give us an extended trial period, maybe up to 60 days. So technically, we wouldn't own the boat until after that. It stays registered to the charter company for the trial period. But if we don't keep it after the trial, we'd forfeit a good bit of the purchase price."

"I'm not worried about the financial side of this. Hiding our ownership's way more important."

"That's what I thought. That's my day," Mary said. "Tell me about yours. I saw you dumped your stuff in the room before I got back from the charter company. How did you manage that?"

"I didn't want Kelley's surveillance people to see me leaving

Island Girl with a lot of luggage. I left her anchored off Fort Recovery and took the dinghy ashore. There's a main road not too far from the shoreline; I flagged down a bus to Road Harbour, then got a taxi to bring me back here."

"Then you took the boat back to the marina?"

"Yes. After I messed around out there for a while. I was giving the new fiberglass in the bilge time to cure. Then I flooded the bilge to float all the gunk up from the bottom of the sump and let it settle over the repair. Once there was a layer of sludge over the new fiberglass, I drained it again. But I was careful not to disturb the sludge. Then I took her back to the marina."

"When Kelley's people notice you're not hanging out on the boat, they'll ask the people in the office about it. How much time do you figure you bought us?"

"Hard to say. I told the people in the office I was going to do some serious hiking around the BVI. I asked them about trails on all the larger islands, and ferries to get around. They'll remember that. And the name they have is Jerome Finnegan. That's the only name Kelley has for me, so they won't be looking for Mr. and Mrs. Fincastle. Or Mary Jordan."

"What about the vessel documentation?" she asked. Mary didn't miss much.

"Finnegan."

"I thought that was the name on the *Carib Princess* document."

"Yes. I have a collection of several documents for the *Island Girl* name to match my different identities. One has Finnegan as the owner, another's for a Delaware corporation. I left the Finnegan one on the chart table with the ship's papers, since that's the name Kelley has."

"We're in good shape, then," she said.

I nodded. "Pretty good. I take it you're interested in hanging out in the islands for a while. That right?"

"Because of wanting a boat?"

"Uh-huh. What's your plan? You still working your way through those files?"

"You said Nora told you I'd been busy. Did she give you any details?"

"Yes. She didn't share any names, but she said O'Hanlon's rumored associates were being methodically wiped out. Said the FBI thinks there's a mob war going on over his turf."

Mary laughed.

"What's funny?"

"Mob war. Nobody ever called me a mob war before."

"Is it over?" I asked.

"The mob war?" She grinned. "Those things never end. Sometimes they wind down for a while."

"Why did this one wind down?"

"There's nobody left on my shit list except a bunch of crooked politicians, and I don't want the heat that goes with that kind of thing. Besides, their street soldiers are all dead, so the politicians are no threat, at least for now."

That's good to hear. Goes a long way toward answering my questions about that gray area.

"You said you wanted my help."

"I do."

"Why, if you're standing down?"

"Personal reasons," she said, giving me a look that made my pulse race. "And to watch my back."

"Sounds good. I like watching your back."

"But what about your friend *Nora*?"

"I told you, there's nothing personal between us." I felt my face flush.

Mary giggled. "Sorry. I couldn't resist teasing you a little. But seriously, what does she want from us?"

"I've been wondering that myself. We'll have to ask her, but my best guess is that it has something to do with those politicians you mentioned."

"Really? I figured they'd be off limits to people like you and Nora. You think that's why she wants me on board?"

That gave me pause. I rubbed my chin, buying a second or two. "I didn't think of that. But you're right. They're seriously off limits for me and Nora; there are non-lethal ways to deal with crooked politicians."

"Just for the record, Finn," Mary started, but I interrupted.

"There's no record here. Not between you and me."

She smiled. "I know that. But between you and me, I'm not interested in doing the government's dirty work. Not if it comes to people who are no threat to me. I've never killed anybody who wouldn't have done the same to me, given the chance. And I'm not about to start now."

"We're together on that, then. I'm relieved to hear you say it, though. I was pretty sure you felt that way."

She nodded. "Okay. That doesn't make me a Girl Scout. Just so there's no misunderstanding between us, I've got connections to some unsavory characters, but they're based on mutual respect, sort of."

"Sort of?"

"Tacit understandings that we won't go after one another — unless there's a good reason. 'Live and let live' is a corollary of sorts to 'kill or be killed,' in my line of work."

"And mine. I understand."

"Good. I'm glad we've talked through all this," Mary said. "I trust you, but I'm not sure about this Nora woman. Do you think she's out to expose the corruption we've found?"

"I wondered about that. But that's a big change from the work we do. Assassination and investigation are different skills."

Mary laughed. "Now that sounds like something a government bureaucrat would say. To a self-employed entrepreneur like me, the distinction's not that clear. I would be comfortable helping her expose those bastards, even though I won't kill them for her. Unless they provoke me, of course."

"Of course," I said. "We'll ask Nora about it. Then we can decide."

"Do you have a secure way to communicate with her, since she's been fired?"

"Yes. She gave me a new satellite phone after I destroyed the old one."

"You destroyed it? Why?"

"She sent me a text warning me it was compromised. She's got one that's the mate to the new one. Both off the books, strictly between the two of us, but the same technology. They'll only connect with each other, same as the old ones."

"So she still has access to that kind of stuff," Mary said.

"In our world, Nora's and mine, that is, an awful lot of things happen based on personal relationships. We all know the government considers us expendable, so we look out for one another."

"You have people you could call on besides her?"

"Yes, but only for certain things, technical stuff, mostly. Like when I got your passport."

"She knew about that, though."

"But only because I told the person who got it that it was okay to treat it as official business. If I told him it was personal, he wouldn't have passed it on to her."

"Why didn't you treat it as personal?"

"I was still trying to figure you out. Letting him tell her was an underhanded way to get them to check you out."

"And did they?"

"Of course. You could have been a big risk to one of their valuable assets."

"Do you know what they learned about me?"

"Yes. In Nora's words, 'Nothing she didn't mean for us to discover.'"

Mary grinned. "So I did well covering my tracks, at least for an amateur, huh?"

"Yeah, but I don't think anybody would mistake you for an amateur."

Mary smiled. "You're sweet."

"I'm serious. You're the best I've run across in 20 years."

She reached across the table and grasped my hand. By then, we were finished with dinner.

"You want dessert?" I asked.

"Yes. But not here. Take me to our room, sailor."

I left enough cash on the table to cover our dinner, with a generous tip. No way I was going to wait for a check after seeing the hunger in her eyes.

25

DRESSED LIKE ALL THE OTHER TOURISTS, MARY AND I ATTRACTED no attention as we got off the ferry from Tortola. We walked to the customs and immigration desk in Red Hook, St. Thomas, and showed our passports. I was supposed to meet Nora at a nearby beach resort.

Before we went to sleep last night, I checked the satellite phone and found a message from her. She asked me to meet her this morning; I was to give her a call a few minutes before I arrived at the resort so she could give me the room number. I was a little anxious because part of her message didn't make sense. She closed with: *Don't get too excited. Missing you a lot, but still sore from last time.*

Aside from the ribbing I got from Mary about that, it worried me. I didn't do anything in St. Martin to make her sore, either literally or otherwise.

Nora only sent the most concise texts; the teasing tone of this one worried me. It might be a covert warning, but I couldn't decipher it.

Once out of the fenced area enclosing the ferry terminal, we were only minutes from the beach resort. I keyed all the necessary digits into the phone, and Nora answered.

"Finn?"

"Yes. I should be there in a few minutes."

"Okay. I ended up in a villa. It's unit 3A, on the beach. Are you alone?"

"Yes."

"Good. Hurry."

With that, she disconnected, and I put the phone in my backpack.

Mary had been standing close, her head next to mine. "What do you think?" she asked.

"She sounded stressed," I said.

"That's what I thought, but I don't know her voice. She sounded congested, like maybe she'd been crying."

We got in a taxi and agreed to an exorbitant fare for the short trip. We could have walked, but arriving in a taxi helped hide where we came from. Mary asked the driver to drop her at a row of tourist shops just outside the entrance to the resort property.

"See you in a few," she said. "Don't forget to call me when you're checked in."

I nodded, and the driver took me to the main entrance to the hotel. I settled with him and got out.

Before I went inside, I took a moment to make sure my cellphone was connected to Mary's, and I muted the speaker. She could hear what was going on around me, but she couldn't talk to me. That was what she meant about calling her after I checked in. I slipped the phone back in the front pocket of my jeans and hoped for the best as I got out of the taxi.

I paused in the lobby for a look at the map of the property. Spotting the villas on the diagram, I leaned down to pick out 3A. The detached villas each housed two suites, and 3A appeared to offer beach access from its patio. Once through the lobby, I followed the signs and soon saw where I was going.

At my knock, the door was opened by a burly man pointing a pistol at me. I registered the suppressor on the muzzle as he pushed it against my belly. *Amateur.* I decided to let him keep his gun, for now.

Nora was tied to a straight chair in the middle of the room, her clothes shredded and bloody. Her head was covered in a black cloth bag. Another thug held a pistol to her head.

"Come in, Finn," Special Agent Kelley said. He was sitting in an easy chair a few feet in front of Nora, his back to me. "Don't do anything stupid, and you'll get to walk out of here in a few minutes."

"I'm sorry, Finn," Nora mumbled through the cloth. "I tried to — "

The thug guarding her swiped his pistol across her hidden face. Her head snapped back from the blow, but she was so far gone she barely flinched.

"Don't worry about it, Nora," I said. "It'll be all right soon."

Kelley laughed and got to his feet, turning to face me. "I'll keep it simple, Finn. I want two things from you in the next 24 hours. Deliver, and you'll live to fight another day. Understand?"

"So far, yeah," I said. "What two things?"

"Thing one, I want your little girlfriend. Thing two, I want the files she stole." He showed me a microSD card in the palm of his hand, the one Nora and I had copied the files to, probably. "They're classified; you know what that means, I'm sure. And I want all the copies. You turn over your laptop and the microSD card the girl has. We'll be able to tell if you've run any copies of either one. If you have, bring the media you copied them to. If you don't have them any longer, I'll need the names and addresses of the people you've shared them with. If I find out you made copies and didn't tell me, I'll hunt you down and make you sorry. Understand?"

"Yeah, I got it. But when I give you the girl and the files, Nora goes free. You won't need her for leverage once you've got what you want."

Kelley laughed and looked toward Nora and the man holding the pistol to her head. "Now, Gregory," Kelley said.

The man's suppressed pistol coughed, and Nora's head exploded inside the cloth bag.

"That was just to show you I'm serious, Finn. I've got leverage you can't even imagine, son. You have 24 hours to get your shit together. Keep your cellphone charged. You'll need it for the delivery instructions. Now get your sorry — "

Kelley was interrupted by the crash of a patio chair coming through the sliding glass door. Before it even hit the floor, Mary was through the opening. She shot the man closest to me first, then the one who killed Nora. Kelley didn't manage to draw his pistol from his shoulder holster before she put rounds in each of his shoulders. That knocked him down, and she stepped closer to him.

"You wanted to meet me, Special Agent Kelley. You got your wish. You're a lucky man. You know why?"

"N-no. I — "

"Because I'm in a hurry. That's why you're lucky. Otherwise I'd make you pay for what you did to the woman. But now I don't have time to waste listening to you scream. Nice meeting you."

She shot him in the forehead. Taking a rag from her shoulder bag, she wiped the pistol she used and bent over the body of the man closest to me. She took his pistol and dropped it in her bag. Using the rag, she put her pistol in his hand and wrapped his fingers around the grip.

"Let's go," she said, grabbing me by the hand and leading me out the shattered sliding door. We walked hand-in-hand down the beach, moving at a pace that indicated we were out for exercise, but not hurrying enough to attract attention.

"Disconnect our phone call," she said, reaching into her bag for her own phone.

"Thanks. I forgot. That trick worked pretty well. Good idea you had."

I took my phone out of my pocket and pressed the red icon.

She watched, frowning, but didn't say anything as I put the phone away again.

"Something wrong?" I asked.

"Disappointed that I didn't move faster. That's all. Poor Nora."

"Where'd you get the pistol?" I asked, after a moment.

She nudged me, turning into the next resort along the beach. We sat down at a table with an umbrella and ordered two glasses of fruit punch.

While the waitress went to get our drinks, Mary answered my question about the pistol. "One of my neighbors at the Fiddler's Green left it in the stairwell."

"He left it? For you?"

"Close enough. He dropped it when I broke his arm. He wanted to be an armed robber, but he was unclear on the concept."

"I see."

The waitress delivered our drinks. "Are you staying here in the resort?" she asked, as she set the glasses on the table with a check.

"No, just out for a stroll along the beach," Mary said.

"Nice morning for it. Thanks for stopping in."

"Thanks," Mary said, taking a sip of her punch as I paid the waitress.

"Just let me know if you guys need a refill," the woman said, smiling.

Once she was gone again, Mary said, "Let's take a taxi downtown and kill a couple of hours, in case somebody's smart enough to watch the ferry terminal."

We drained our glasses, and I nodded. We both stood and walked through the lobby to the front door, where there was a taxi waiting for a fare. We got in and told the driver we wanted to go to Fort Christian in Charlotte Amalie.

He nodded. "You like this hotel?" he asked.

"Yes. It's really nice," Mary said.

"Where you folks from?"

"The States," Mary said. She slid across the seat to snuggle against me, turning her face up for a kiss to give the driver a clue that we weren't looking for conversation.

As we pulled out onto the main road, an ambulance and two police cars roared by, sirens screaming. Our driver shook his head.

"Drugs. Almos' always drugs behind that kind of t'ing."

"Nowhere's safe anymore," I said, breaking off our lingering kiss.

"Amen," Mary said, crossing herself.

I took her hand and gave it a squeeze. She turned her face up to mine again, her lips parted in anticipation.

26

THE DRIVER LET US OUT AT THE SIDEWALK LEADING UP TO FORT Christian, and we merged with the crowd of tourists. Strolling through the fort, studying the placards that described its history, we let 15 minutes pass.

"Let's go find somewhere to have a nice long lunch," I suggested. "Then by the time we get back to Red Hook, the ferry will be crowded. Safety in numbers."

"Sounds good to me," she said, as we made our way out of Fort Christian. "You have anywhere in mind?"

"No. Let's walk until something strikes your fancy."

She nodded and took my hand, weaving her fingers through mine. Once we were clear of the crowd exiting Fort Christian, she looked over at me and asked, "You okay about Nora?"

I shrugged. "Comes with the job, I guess."

"I know you said there wasn't anything between you — romance, I mean — but 20 years is a long time. It's okay to feel bad for her; you won't upset me if you need to mourn her."

I stopped and tugged her hand, turning her to face me. Leaning toward her, I planted a kiss on her lips. "Thanks. It may hit me later; I don't know. But I appreciate your kindness."

She smiled. "It feels good," she said, as we started walking again.

"Feels good?"

"Just being with you, walking along and holding hands. I've never had anybody like you, anybody that... I don't even know where to start."

"Yeah," I said. "Me either. It does feel good. By the way, thanks for saving my ass this morning, speaking of new experiences."

"I'm glad I could help. Sorry I didn't read the situation well enough to save Nora."

"Don't second guess yourself. Even being in the room with them, I didn't see that coming. I was as surprised as they were when you crashed through the door. Having backup's something new for me."

"I know. Me, too. I like having a partner, Finn."

"Good. I like it, too. It's still strange. But thanks again for saving me."

"You're welcome, but we both know you'd have been fine without me. I saw you getting set to attack right before I threw the chair through that glass door. Those two guys were newbies. I was tempted just for a minute to watch you take his gun away."

"Glad you didn't wait."

"But I'm curious. Were you going to shoot him first? The guy closest to you?"

"No. The one who shot Nora would have been number one. Kelley would have been two. I would have knocked the one closest to me out with a head butt when I took his pistol. I was moving around to put him between me and the others when you broke the sliding glass door."

"Nice plan. I wondered."

"Did you think to pick up the microSD card Kelley took from Nora?" I asked. "I missed that in the excitement."

"No. I thought about it, but I decided to leave it. Maybe it'll fall into the hands of somebody who's not crooked. A little exposure might be good for these bastards."

"Might be," I said. "I didn't expect that Kelley was going to come after us like he did. Any idea what prompted that?"

"No, not really. I don't see how they could have known I was here. And he gave you 24 hours to get me here, so he probably didn't know. You see any signs that point to a different conclusion?"

"No, except for Nora."

"What about her?"

"I'm wondering how Kelley even knew about her. You already know as much about her as I do. That's precious little. He managed to find her, but how?"

"You said she got in trouble for asking about him. Think that might have gotten back to him, somehow?"

"You mean, somebody up the line blew her cover?"

"Yes. Could that be?"

"It could, but that's a scary thought. Besides whoever else there is like me, I can only think of three people who even knew she existed. But I didn't know enough to blow her cover, so I have to figure the other operators like me wouldn't, either."

"You won't like this, Finn. But I'm going to ask, anyway."

"You can guess the one at the top. The next one down is — "

She put a finger to my lips. "That's not what I was going to ask."

I frowned, shaking my head. "What, then?"

"You think she could have been part of it?"

"Part of it? You mean could Nora have been paid off? Gone rogue? I don't — "

"Don't rush into that. I know what your knee-jerk reaction

is. Think about it while we have lunch. Give it time to percolate."

I chewed on the inside of my cheek and nodded. She could be on to something.

"Okay," I said. "I'll do that."

"This looks like a good place to eat and kill a little time," she said, breaking her stride.

We studied the menu taped in the window of what looked to be an upscale seafood restaurant.

"Suits me," I said.

"Let's don't talk about her while we eat, okay?"

"Okay," I said. "Better not to rush it, for sure. Good idea to let it percolate, like you said."

"Yes, and besides, it spoils my fantasy."

"Fantasy?" I asked, raising my eyebrows.

She tugged my hand, moving me into the restaurant, ignoring my unspoken question.

"Table for two?" the hostess asked.

"Yes, please," Mary said. "Something private, for me and my husband. We're on our honeymoon."

The hostess smiled. "I've got just the spot for you — a nice, secluded booth in the back. Follow me, please."

After the hostess seated us and left, I asked, "Husband? Honeymoon?"

"Part of my fantasy. I've always wanted to say that. Does it make you nervous?"

I thought about that for a second, watching the emotions play across her face. "No. No, not even a little bit. Tell me more about this fantasy of yours."

"Later. I promise. But I don't want to break the spell by talking about it right now. Okay?"

"Okay," I said, feeling an uncontrollable grin spread over my face. "I'm glad you're letting me share your fantasy."

"Oh, you're not just sharing it. You're the heart of it. Now, let's talk about where we're going next."

"On our honeymoon," I said. "Where would you like to go next?"

"I've always had the notion that there were islands where there were no other people. Are there any?"

"Oh, yeah. Quite a few, even in this crowded part of the world."

"Then let's explore some of them."

"They're mostly tiny, and they don't have fresh water. That's why they're uninhabited."

"I don't want to live there forever. I just want the experience of not having to watch my back. We could carry enough food and water on the boat to last us for a while, right?"

"Right. Speaking of the boat, maybe we should check out some of the charter operations here on St. Thomas — see what they have for sale."

"You think they'll have something different from what I saw in Tortola?"

I shrugged. "I doubt it. Just an idea. It's something to do to kill time."

"We could, I guess, but I've lost my sense of urgency for a boat, with Kelley out of the game. I'd like to enjoy Cane Garden Bay for a few days. Just kick back and relax, get to know you."

"We've known one another for a good while now," I said.

"Oh, you know what I mean. All those silly courtship rituals are behind us now. Let's take a little time and really get to know one another, now that the pressure's off."

"You think it's going to be that easy?"

"We won't know if we don't give it a try, Finn. I don't need to go back to work. I'm pretty well set for life, and I'm betting you are, too. If not, well, how would you feel about being a kept man?"

"Best offer I've ever had. But I think we better take a look at the menu."

"Hungry?" Mary asked.

"Yes, but besides that, this place is filling up, and the waitress keeps eyeing us, wondering when we're going to order."

"Oh, all right, then. Let's look at the menu." She gave me a look that made my blood pressure skyrocket. Then she smiled and ran her tongue over her lips. "Now that you mention it, I'm in a hurry to get back to our room. Maybe we should skip lunch."

"Your call," I said, trying to keep my voice even.

"On second thought, we should eat. You need to keep your strength up."

"Yes, ma'am," I said, waving the waitress over to our table.

"Ready to order?" she asked.

"Yes," I said. "What's the quickest meal on the menu."

"The quickest... Nobody's ever asked me that before. Are you in a hurry?"

"He's just being silly," Mary said. "Anticipation sharpens the appetite, I'm told."

"Maybe I should tell you about our specials," the waitress said.

"Good. Let's hear them," I said, ignoring that smoldering, liquid look in Mary's eyes.

27

HOVERING IN THAT ODD ZONE BETWEEN SLEEP AND WAKEFULNESS, I was recovering from playing my part in Mary's fantasy. We were stretched out on the bed in our room in Cane Garden Bay. It was late afternoon; we'd been back long enough to... well, you know.

She was asleep, her head resting on my shoulder, when I had one of those breakthrough thoughts that come when they're least expected. At the same moment, Mary woke up.

"Finn?"

"Mm. I thought you were zonked. Are you awake?"

"You jumped; it startled me. I guess I was asleep. Is something wrong?"

"No, but as long as you're awake, I wondered about that pistol — the one you took from Kelley's guy."

"How did you get there?"

"I don't know; I was worried about it, I guess. It just popped into my mind. I didn't know I jumped. Sorry if it woke you up."

"That's okay. What about the pistol?"

"You still have it in your bag?"

"No. I ditched it when we were on the ferry. Why?"

"Good. I didn't see you do that." I turned my head a little, so I could see her face.

She smiled. "No, I don't imagine you did."

"When did you do it?"

"Remember when we were all alone, smooching on the aft deck?"

"How could I forget? But I didn't see you toss it."

She giggled. I've only heard her giggle once or twice; it's out of character.

"You were busy."

"You managed to ditch the pistol *then?*"

Another giggle. "Yes. I figured that if anybody was watching, they wouldn't notice me dropping it over the side. You were providing a great diversion."

"And I thought all that squirming was because you were in the throes of passion."

"That too. Why were you worried about the pistol?"

"I didn't want us to forget to lose it. A found pistol's a dangerous thing to hang onto. No telling what kind of history it might have."

"Yes, you're right about that. Rest easy, though; I took care of it."

"You think somebody was watching us when we were... "

"No, but it never hurts to be cautious," she said. "What time is it, anyway?"

"Don't know. You thinking about dinner?"

"Maybe. I lost track."

Reaching over to the bedside table with my free hand, I picked up my cellphone and pressed the home button. The screen lit up, and I saw that I had a text message.

"Five o'clock," I said, unlocking the phone with my thumb.

"What are you doing?"

"I got a text since we've been back."

"I didn't hear the alert," she said, propping herself up on her elbow.

"Because the phone was still silenced from this morning. I forgot to turn the ringer back on."

"Who's it from?"

"I'm getting there. It's not from a number in my contacts. Hang on."

I held the phone where we could both see the screen and opened the text. The photograph at the beginning sent my heart rate into the stratosphere.

"Who is she, Finn? Her picture's on the bulkhead in the saloon. I didn't want to ask, but I've wondered..."

I was too stunned to respond as I read the text below the photograph.

She's a pretty girl. Don't worry. We won't do anything to spoil her looks. Wouldn't want to reduce her market value. In case our friend in St. Thomas forgot to tell you before he died, we want the girl who was calling herself Mary Elizabeth O'Brien. And we want to know who has copies of the files she stole from the Daileys. You have 48 hours to deliver. After that, we'll send you videos every six hours to keep you up to date on what's happening to this sweet child until you give us what we want. Keep your phone close by.

"Who is she, Finn?" Mary asked, putting a hand on my chest giving me a little nudge.

My mouth was so dry it was hard for me to speak. "My daughter."

"Shit! I'm so sorry. I didn't know. I've brought this on you."

"Not your fault."

"I didn't know you had a daughter."

"I've never even met her. And now, this. They're going to pay; they have no idea."

"I'll go, Finn."

"Go?"

"In her place. Send them a text."

"No. That's not going to solve anything. They won't let her go, anyway."

"Finn?"

"Yeah?"

"Tell me about her."

"I was married when I first went on active duty. She was born while I was on a covert assignment in Afghanistan, before all the shit started over there. I found out about her birth the same time I got the divorce papers. That's about all there is to tell."

"You never met her?"

"That's right. I thought it was best, given my line of work. Because... " I stopped, my voice cracking.

"Because you thought something like this might happen?"

"Yeah."

"Where'd you get the picture?"

"I tracked her down. I wanted to know... "

"Where?"

"Where what?"

"Where did you find her?"

"Oh. I kept track of her all along. I shot that picture that's on the boat not long after she started college. She's at the University of Florida."

"Now?"

"Yeah. Well, now I... "

"You have an address for her? A current address?"

"Yeah."

"Give it to me."

"What? Why?"

"We're going to get her out of this."

"How?"

"Trust me. If she was snatched in Florida, I know someone who can find her. Give me her address. And her name. Hurry, damn it. Time's precious."

I rolled out of bed and dug my laptop out of my duffle bag. My daughter's details were in an encrypted file on the hard drive. In a few seconds, I pulled them up on the screen and turned it where Mary could see it.

She picked up her big shoulder bag and took out a cheap cellphone.

"Burner," she said, seeing me looking at it.

She keyed in a number, and I heard the phone ringing.

"Yeah?" a man's voice asked.

"Medusa," Mary said.

"Wait one."

"Phorcys. To what do I owe the pleasure?" This was another man's voice.

"About that favor you owe me."

"Anything. How may I help?"

"A girl was kidnapped in Gainesville in the last few hours. She's an innocent civilian. Her name's Abigail Edith Carroll." Mary spelled the last name. "Her address is 1701 Southwest 16th Street, Apartment 201."

"Okay, I have that. You want her freed, I take it."

"Yes, please."

"That shouldn't be a problem. Anything else?"

"Yes. Make an example of her captors. But before you finish with them, find out who ordered this."

"Certainly. And then?"

"Put out the word that she's under your protection, in case anyone misses the implication. Let me know who's behind it, and I'll take it from there."

"Excellent. I'll be in touch as soon as Ms. Carroll is safe at home. Is this a good number for you?"

"For now. And this time, I owe you, for a change."

"No. This one's still on me. Gainesville's my turf, as the less savory elements would say. I didn't authorize this. And it's a pleasure to hear from you."

"Likewise. And thanks."

"My pleasure."

She disconnected the call and turned to me. "You heard?"

"Yes. But who is Phorcys?"

"Phorcys and his sister Ceto were Medusa's parents."

"I didn't mean in mythology. Was that your father?"

She frowned. "You mean because I said I was Medusa?"

I nodded.

"It's just a challenge and response we use."

I noticed she evaded my question. "And how do you know this person?"

"I've done some work for him; he feels indebted to me."

"How can he find Abby?"

"I can't answer that, because I don't know. But he will. Nothing happens in Florida's underworld that he doesn't know about. Like you said about Nora, he has a track record with me."

"Okay. I don't know if I can just sit here; I feel so helpless."

"You're not helpless, Finn. I wouldn't want to be the people holding your daughter."

"When you get the name of the person behind this, I'll handle it, just so we're clear on that."

Mary locked eyes with me. "No, partner. *We'll* handle it. You and I. I got us into this; I'm going to do my share to get us out. That's the way this is going to work between us. Got it?"

I nodded, but I'm sure I didn't look happy. I could tell from the expression on her face.

"Finn?"

"What?"

"Does she know you even exist?"

"Abby?"

Mary nodded.

"She... I don't know. I've not heard from her mother since the divorce. There was a court order that prohibited me from having any contact with either of them, in exchange for my having no obligation for child support or alimony."

"You agreed to that?"

"By default. It all happened while I was crawling on my belly in the dust, like some kind of reptile. I was out of touch for almost a year. And then I wasn't coherent for a good while after I rejoined the living. By the time I got my wits about me, it was too late to do anything about it."

"I would think it's never too late, in a situation like that."

"It may not have been, technically. But my ex-wife was remarried, and her new husband adopted Abby. I figured the best thing for everybody was to let it go. That all happened while I was kind of missing in action."

"Kind of?"

"Well, since there was no official U.S. presence where I was and the government was actively denying our involvement at the time... "

"I see. That's so sad, though."

"Well, I decided it was probably best for Abby if I let her have a normal life."

"I understand, but that must've been hard for you."

I shrugged. "I managed."

"Who knows about this? About your having a daughter, I mean."

"I've never mentioned it to a soul, except you. But there are court records, back there somewhere, I guess. And maybe something in my military record." I frowned. "So how in the hell ... "

"My question, exactly. How did these people find out about your daughter to begin with? This is getting scary, Finn. It's surreal."

"Before you came through the sliding door this morning, I was trying to negotiate with Kelley. I argued that once I gave him you and the files, he should let Nora go; he wouldn't need her for leverage. That's when he told the guy to kill her. Then he laughed at me and said, 'I've got leverage you can't even imagine, son.' I was wondering what he meant, but now it's clear. He knew about Abby, knew they had her. Too bad we didn't have time to question him."

"Well, we'll soon know what he could have told us."

"Yeah. But it would have been nice to hear him screaming for a while."

"Let it go, Finn. Abby's going to be fine."

"Part of the 48 hours is already up."

"I'll be surprised if she's not home by morning, wondering what happened," Mary said.

"What will your friend's people tell her?" I asked. "How are they going to explain why somebody snatched her? And who will she think rescued her?"

"Those are valid concerns, but you've skipped some worrisome questions."

"What do you mean?"

"They knew about Nora, and they know Abby's your daughter. How?"

"Damn. You're right. I thought of that and moved right past it. I'm losing it. What's wrong with me?"

"You're not losing it. You would have come back to those points. But there's another thing bothering me, here."

"What's that?"

"All this started because I took those files, Finn."

I frowned.

"Your connection with me is the only reason they're after you — and that led them to Nora and your daughter."

"Maybe so, but that doesn't matter at this point. We're in this together. No point in digging through what-might-have-been-if-only stuff."

"Yes, there is. I'm not doing it to shoulder the blame. There's something wrong here. They got to you way too fast. Think about it. They got to Nora, and she was practically invisible. And your relationship to Abby's buried even deeper."

"Are you saying there's another connection? Besides the one between you and me?"

"You started me down that path when you were talking about who knew about Nora, besides you and her boss. And I guess her boss's boss, maybe. And then you said there might be something in your military records."

"I see where you're going. Whoever gave away Nora and my daughter is probably in my chain of command. With Nora dead, that leaves three people, and the one at the top is unlikely."

"That would be the president?"

"No comment."

"He's just a scum-sucking politician, Finn. Why do you say he's an unlikely candidate?"

"Oh, it's nothing to do with his ethics. He's morally bankrupt; no question about that. It's just that he wouldn't know my name, or even Nora's. He would only know that he could authorize something and that there were people like us who made it happen."

"I see. So you think it's one of the other two?"

"Almost certain to be."

"I don't want to know who they are," Mary said.

"I don't blame you. One of them's a public figure, but even I don't know the other one's name. Nora's boss, that is. And I suspect Nora's operation is only part of his — or her — portfolio."

"Where do you want to go with all this, Finn?"

"I don't know yet. I want Abby safe. When your friend tells us who gave the order, maybe we'll see a little deeper into the swamp. What are you planning to do once we have the name?"

"I was planning to talk that over with you, partner. But if it were up to me, I'd kill the bastard without blinking an eye. I'd question him first, though."

"Yeah. I think we're missing something."

"What's that?" Mary asked.

"About those files. I took a look, but they didn't make sense. Now that we've got a better idea of who we're looking for, maybe the two of us should revisit them."

"Okay by me. But can we get dressed and go get something to eat first?"

"Yes. Let's go."

28

"IT MUST HAVE BEEN HARD FOR YOU, KNOWING ABOUT ABBY AND keeping your distance," Mary said.

We were strolling along the waterfront in Cane Garden Bay, walking off our dinner. The restaurant was crowded enough to deprive us of privacy, but now we were alone.

I looked at Mary, wondering what was on her mind. Before I could ask, her next comment told me she knew what I was thinking.

"I mean, I know you care about her; you wouldn't have had her picture on the boat, otherwise. Weren't you ever tempted to meet her anonymously, somehow?"

"Yes. But Abby's life is normal. I didn't want to risk taking that away from her. I only came close to crossing the line once. She was the valedictorian of her high school class. She got all kinds of scholastic recognition and was written up in their local paper. The story mentioned how tough it was going to be for her to afford college. Her adopted dad developed serious health problems; the family finances were in the pits."

"So you're paying for college?"

"Yes. Through a blind trust."

"How well insulated are you?"

"Bulletproof. I went through an offshore bank, and even there I used an identity that our government didn't know about."

"You certain about that?"

I shrugged. "Yes, but I was certain about my connection to Nora being hidden, too. I was wrong about one or the other, I guess."

"Or both," Mary said.

"Or both." I held the door for her as we walked into the lobby of our hotel. "Nightcap?"

"Not unless you need one. Let's call it a night. We may have a busy day tomorrow. I've got a feeling we're going to Florida."

"I know you haven't heard from your friend since you called him. What makes you think Florida?" I let us in our room.

"A gut feeling. Your daughter was snatched in Florida. There are all kinds of Florida connections in this mess. There's no reason I can see for her kidnappers to move her out of the state."

"You really think your friend will find her that fast? Tomorrow?"

"I'd be surprised if he didn't, so we should be ready to move in a hurry."

I grimaced and shook my head. "As much as I want to, I can't rush to her side to comfort her as soon as she's safe, Mary. She's already going to be traumatized. I'd just add to her confusion."

"I understand. That's not what I meant."

"You think whoever ordered this is in Florida?"

"Good chance. All the bad guys I've tangled with so far were in Florida."

"I thought O'Hanlon was from Boston."

"*From* is the right word. He spent all his time at his villa in one of the upscale golf communities the Daileys built."

"What about the people they were bribing?"

"That's a different story; they're everywhere."

"Everywhere? You're exaggerating, right?"

Mary shrugged and smiled at me. "No. When I was trying to decipher who was on the take, I got overwhelmed in a hurry. There are too many for them all to be in Florida. But the out-and-out criminals are concentrated there."

"How much were you able to get out of the files? I couldn't make any sense of them. You said something about context, and Nora thought she could get people to help, but that's off the table, now."

"I couldn't get names. Those are all encrypted. But the files were a standard format, so I combined them into one big spreadsheet. That way, I could sort them different ways. I was hoping to spot patterns."

"I'm surprised the whole files weren't encrypted. Why only the names of the people getting paid?"

"I can't answer that. Maybe it made the data too hard to work with. Or the Daileys were just overconfident about their physical security. They had the only copies of the files; they were all in that safe. O'Hanlon told me that going in, and the Daileys confirmed it when I questioned them."

"Could you tell anything about the names? Like an indication of the encryption scheme?"

"Not yet. Maybe if I could get one name and match it against something else in the files, then I could at least see the encrypted version of the name. That might give us a clue. You see another way?"

"Maybe. It depends on how good their code is. There are standard ways to crack simple codes. If they didn't bother to encrypt the whole set of files, I'll bet they didn't use anything too complicated for the names."

"Do you want to give it a try?" Mary asked.

"Not just yet. You said you combined the files into one database so you could sort the entries. What did you discover?"

"Nothing I could use, but there were a couple of interesting things that popped out at me."

"What popped out?"

"The first thing I did was sort on the 'payee name' column. That collected all the payments to the same person in a sequence, by date. That's useless so far, but it also showed thousands of payees."

"Thousands? Like two thousand, or ten thousand?"

"I didn't count; I got overwhelmed, like I said. Some names had close to a hundred payments. So even counting them was daunting. I know there's a way to do that using the software, but I didn't get there yet."

"That's a hell of a list," I said. "No wonder so many people want it. It may not be *every* corrupt politician in the country, but it must be most of the ones that matter. Do you know who any of them are? Got any educated guesses?"

"Not really. Why?"

"I'm thinking about how to crack the code. The more names we have, the quicker it will go. Known participants would be better than guesses, but guesses might get us started. Think about it like trying to solve a crossword puzzle."

"Do you know how to crack codes, Finn?"

"I know a little about it, on a conceptual level. Less about the mechanics of doing it. But I have a contact. Maybe."

"Like the person who got that passport for me?"

"Like that, yes."

"Do you trust this person? The code cracker? Because the passport person told Nora, right?"

"Yes, but I didn't ask him not to tell her. That was an underhanded way for me to get them to check you out. I told you that.

I figured if you were bad news, they'd warn me. But to answer your question, I wouldn't give the person the files."

"I don't understand how it would work, then."

"I'd give them a big enough sample of the encrypted names to work with. We know that we're looking for people's names, not numeric data.

"They'll analyze the encrypted data from the name field. The tools use statistics on the frequency of occurrence for different letters as they appear in people's names. That will give us some encoding schemes ranked in order of the most likely fit."

"You're giving me a headache, Finn. How's that going to help us?"

"We'll try the different possible encoding schemes on our list of known payees. Once we get it right, then we can use a macro on the spreadsheet file to convert the encrypted names to plain English."

"Then what?" Mary asked.

"Then you and I can decide what we want to do with the list. If it's dangerous now, imagine how dangerous it'll be when it's not encrypted."

"You thinking blackmail?"

"Not interested. I've got plenty of money, and you said the same thing earlier. But we'll have the leverage to protect ourselves, if nothing else."

Mary was frowning.

"What's wrong?"

"Just sorry we left that microSD card with Kelley's body."

"I wouldn't worry too much about it. By the time it's in the hands of somebody who knows what to do with it, this will probably be over."

"You sound optimistic, Finn."

"Yeah. I'm trying not to think about Abby."

"She's in good hands. Trust me on that."

"I'm working on it."

"Think you can sleep with all this on your mind?" Mary asked, as she turned out the light.

"Yes. That's a learned skill in my trade. Sleep's a weapon. Good night."

29

I GRABBED MY CELLPHONE FROM THE NIGHTSTAND, STARTLED from sleep. Fumbling with it, I saw that it was a little after 4 a.m. At first, I thought I missed the call that woke me.

Then I heard Mary say, "Medusa." It was her burner phone that rang. She put a finger over my lips and switched her phone to speaker mode. I nodded.

"Phorcys. Can you talk?"

"Yes."

"The young woman you called about yesterday is at home, safe in her own bed."

"Thank you. That was fast. Is she all right?"

"Yes. She's unharmed, and she's not likely to remember any of what happened. They picked the lock on her front door and waited for her to come home. Then they injected her with flunitrazepam in her own living room before she even knew they were there. They never moved her from her apartment."

"Flunitra... what?" Mary asked.

"Commonly called 'Roofies.'"

"I thought Roofies were pills."

"Yes. Or the powder can be dissolved in distilled water and injected. Less common, but it has the same result."

"So she won't know what happened to her?"

"That's correct."

"And what about the men who took her?"

"They've been dealt with. They were quite forthcoming, actually. Two contract intelligence operatives — not your garden variety thugs at all, fortunately for the girl. They took good care of her on instructions from their superiors. Professionals to the end."

"Who were their superiors?"

"They're being taken care of as we speak. Don't concern yourself with them. The person you're interested in is none other than our favorite elected official."

"Really? The one we were hoping to *vote out*?"

The man on the phone chuckled. "The same. I can handle that now, if you wish."

"No, I don't think so. This is personal, but thank you."

"As you wish. Let me know if you change your mind, or if you need anything. All the damning material is in place, ready for release once the news of his suicide breaks. I look forward to reading about him in the news soon."

"I really do owe you for this."

"No. The balance is still in your favor. Perhaps someday I'll need to call on you, but for now you owe me nothing. Stay well, Medusa."

There was a click as he disconnected, and Mary turned to me. "You heard everything?"

"Yes. Who's the elected official?"

"A high-level Florida politician I suspected of taking payoffs from Dailey and O'Hanlon. He's the next step up the chain from the out-and-out crooks I eliminated."

"He got a name?"

"Jefferson Davis Lee. Ring a bell?"

"The Senator? Hell yes, it rings a bell. Mr. Law and Order himself."

"That's the one. You know about his committee affiliation?"

"I know he's on the Senate Armed Services Committee."

"Yes. Would that put him in a position to know about Nora's little business?"

"I don't think so, but like I said earlier, I'm not sure of anything at this stage. You think he's dirty?"

"I do now. I wasn't sure before. He looked dirty, but I couldn't prove it. If the Daileys and O'Hanlon weren't paying *him*, they were paying somebody with the same connections."

"Why did you suspect him before this? You said all the names in the files were encrypted."

"My friend Phorcys thought Lee was taking money from somebody. But he wasn't certain."

"Why did he think that?"

"Because Lee has all the earmarks of a crooked politician, but he ignored several chances to pick up some serious cash."

"Are you saying your friend offered to buy him and struck out?"

"I don't know that. Don't jump to conclusions about my friend. Somebody — my friend didn't say who — made Lee offers that he turned down. So we figured Lee was already bought and paid for."

"You mentioned there was nobody left on your shit list except crooked politicians. Is Lee one of them?"

"Yes. He was the next in line. I declared a unilateral cease-fire when I came to him."

"Because you weren't sure about him?"

"That, plus there's the matter of appearances."

"Appearances?"

"Gangsters get killed all the time, and nobody pays much attention. If you're into hunting metaphors, killing gangsters is like varmint hunting. Crooked politicians are a different kind of game; they're like hunting an endangered species."

"Bullshit. They're not endangered. They're more numerous than English sparrows."

Mary laughed. "You're right; I should have said 'protected,' not 'endangered.' But you get my point."

"Yes. You're worried about the heat that might come from killing a senator. And you said the politicians weren't an immediate threat anyway, since they didn't have any foot soldiers left. So you decided not to go after Lee?"

"It's not that simple, but you're on the right track. I just needed to wait. There are ways to hunt protected species without unleashing a furor, but they have to be taken on an individual basis, like rogue tigers. If politicians are known crooks, nobody is surprised when they're taken down."

"How about Lee?"

"He isn't a known crook. Not yet, anyway. But we plan to change that."

"Is that what your friend meant by the 'damning material?'"

"Yes. When Lee commits suicide, there won't be any doubt about why he did it."

"Suicide, as opposed to an accident or a robbery gone wrong. That was already decided?"

"Yes. We were already building the history to support it, even before Lee ordered your daughter's kidnapping."

"I see. And your friend will release evidence of Lee's taking bribes? That's supposed to explain his suicide?"

"It won't be that straight-forward, but you've got the idea. Ordinary corruption has become the norm for mainstream politicians in recent years. Nobody would bat an eye at Lee's taking bribes. They all do that. Some kind of extreme sexual perversion is a more credible reason for a guy like Lee to kill himself. Maybe it's about to come out that he's a serial rapist, or a child molester. But I'm just guessing."

Who is this Phorcys character? And what's your connection with him? How did Lee know about your relationship with me? And how did any of them know about Abby? Or Nora? There's a lot of coincidence, here, especially since you and Phorcys already planned to kill Lee.

"If Lee's going to commit suicide, I guess we can't interrogate him first."

"We might be able to, within limits."

"How?"

"Think drugs, Finn. A guy like that will choose pills or dope for his exit; he wouldn't have the guts to shoot himself or slash his wrists. If he's found with a lethal dose of several different drugs in his system, who's to say which ones he took first? Not being a druggie, he probably scarfed down whatever he could get his hands on."

I nodded. "Guess we should pack; we should be able to get seats on a flight from St. Thomas to Miami this morning."

"We've got a little time. The first ferry won't leave for a couple of hours, yet."

"What do you have in mind?" I asked.

She put her arms around my neck. "Might as well make the most of our time alone," she said.

"Mmf," I said, her lips muffling my response.

30

THE MIAMI FLIGHT WAS CROWDED ENOUGH SO THAT MARY AND I couldn't talk about our plans. That was okay with me; it gave me time to think. I was troubled by the loose ends surrounding our situation.

The biggest question in my mind was how these people found out about me. I don't mean my relationship with Mary; when I first took up with her several weeks ago, I thought I was using her for camouflage. That was humorous, given what I learned in the last few hours. I chuckled.

"What's funny, Finn?"

"Life."

"Life's funny?"

"Yeah. It's full of ironic twists."

"Like what?"

"If I told you, I'd have to — "

"Yeah, yeah," she said, smiling. "But tell me later, okay?"

"I will. I promise."

She went back to the novel she was reading on her iPhone, leaving me to my thoughts. I picked up where I left off. Mary was camouflage, all right, but I got sucked right into her life in the bargain. That was okay. Her life wasn't all that much different from mine. Only the other players were different. Or were they?

During the last few days, the casts of characters in our separate dramas merged. I couldn't account for the extent of Nora's knowledge about Mary. And I couldn't ask Nora about it at this point.

Thinking of Nora reminded me that I was in limbo. She was my only contact within my client organization. There were a few other people I could call, but they were in supporting roles. They were the people who could arrange new identities for me, or break codes... That was another loose end.

I still needed to get a sample of the encrypted names from Mary's files. My laptop was in my carry-on bag; maybe I could do that if we had idle time this evening. I didn't want to get wrapped up in that until we settled on how to deal with our current target. He was the one who ordered Abby's kidnapping, and presumably Nora's murder.

Which brought me back around to my daughter and Nora. I couldn't talk to Nora, but I planned to call Abby. Once we were on the ground in Miami, I would pick up a burner cellphone and call her, just to hear her voice. Mary's friend Phorcys said she was sleeping off her drugs, so there was no big hurry. But I wanted to know she was well before our encounter with the senator.

And who the hell was Phorcys? When I asked Mary, she was evasive, at least about her relationship with him.

In mythology, Phorcys was Medusa's father. But in mythology, Medusa had snakes instead of hair, so it didn't pay to put too much stock in mythology. But there was that tattoo of Medusa on Mary's hip...

Whoever Phorcys was, he seemed to owe Mary favors, and he could deliver when she called them in. That was important, but it also made me wonder why he was so helpful to her. That was another loose end.

And yet another loose end — with Nora dead, who would relay instructions to me?

No doubt someone would take Nora's place, and that someone would have enough information to establish her (or maybe his) bona fides with me. Until then, though, I was a free agent. I suspected that I would remain so until this whole mess was cleared up.

Since I didn't know about Nora's official status, I couldn't even guess about when she would be missed. And speaking of Nora, I wondered if she *was* part of the corruption, as Mary suggested a while back. Somebody told the bad guys about my daughter. They almost certainly found out from somebody in my chain of command.

I already narrowed the suspects down to Nora or her immediate boss. The implications of that were disturbing. I worked for those two for almost twenty years, and one of them was probably compromised. But which one, and for how long?

On the strength of their orders, a lot of people died at my hands. My targets deserved what they got. I knew enough about each of them to feel comfortable with what I did at the time. But after seeing Mary and Phorcys set up the senator, there was a scintilla of doubt in my mind. Had I been manipulated by Nora and company?

For that matter, was I being manipulated by Mary?

31

"Did you reach Abby?" Mary asked, as I backed our rental car out of its parking place.

"Yes. She sounded okay. Maybe a little confused, but okay." I called Abby on my new burner phone while Mary was arranging for the car and checking in with her friend.

"Who did you tell her you were?"

"I gave her a yarn about being part of a non-denominational campus outreach ministry, trying to make sure every student had a spiritual home."

"Are you kidding?"

"No. I was shooting for something innocuous that might let me engage her in a little conversation, just to make sure about her. Told her we provided counseling services, and that she could call us any time she felt the need."

"What did she say to that?"

"She asked me, 'Who the hell gave you this number? It's unlisted. Is this a scam?'"

Mary laughed. "Sounds like my kind of gal. What did you tell her?"

"I told her an acquaintance of hers was worried because she

tried to call Abby last night and couldn't get an answer when she knew Abby was home. I spun that out a little; told her the girl walked by her place and saw the lights on, but nobody answered her knock on the door."

"She must have asked you who it was."

"Yes. I told her the person requested anonymity."

"What did she say to that?"

"She was confused, like I said. But she got irritated. Told me she thought I was a crank caller, and not to bother her anymore."

"She sounds okay to me."

"Well, I don't know; I've never talked to her before."

"No?"

"No."

"How did you recognize her voice?"

"From her answering machine. I've called before when I knew she was in class, just to hear her voice."

"If I didn't know you better, I'd think you were some pathetic creep."

"Thanks, Mary. I felt like a creep. But I... well, it was the only way I could think of to have a little contact with her."

"I'm sorry, Finn. I know you're not a creep. That whole situation is just so sad. You should make an effort to have a real relationship with her. She's not a child anymore; she could handle it."

"You think so?"

"What's the downside? Rejection?"

"Yes."

"How is that worse than what you have now?"

"Now at least I can hope that someday I'll..."

"You'll what?"

I shook my head, stopping at the exit from the rental car lot and lowering the window. The guard reached in for the contract and checked the license number on the car.

"Thank you, sir. Have a good day, and drive safely." She returned the rental agreement and opened the gate for us.

As I pulled out into traffic, Mary asked, "Have you thought about talking with your ex-wife about this?"

"About establishing a relationship with Abby? You're kidding, right?"

"No. Your marriage crashed and burned, but you share a daughter. You both care about her. Maybe your ex would have some thoughts."

"Or tell me to get lost."

"For a tough guy, you can be pretty timid, Finn. Think about it, anyway. Okay?"

"Okay. Why do you care?"

"Because I can see that you care about Abby. She's a lucky girl to have a father like you, and she doesn't even know it. I'd like to see the two of you make each other happy."

"I'll think about it. Right now, we've got other stuff to deal with. You talked to your friend while I was getting the phone?"

"I did, yes. Lee is in town; the Senate's in recess. All we need is to figure out how to get him alone for a little while."

"He married?"

"Sort of. He and his wife don't spend much time together. She's not here with him, if that's what you're asking."

"So he's a bachelor, for now. Where does he live?"

"He has a house about twenty minutes from here, in a fancy, gated community that the Daileys developed."

"That figures, doesn't it?"

"Yes. His place looks out over a golf course. It's nice and private, not a bad place for us to visit him."

"That sounds too convenient."

"It does. There's a problem, though. He has a mistress here; she has her own condo in the same development."

"Cozy. Where's he spending his evenings? With her? Or at home?"

"Mostly with her. But he's back and forth between his place and hers. He entertains donors and friends at his house and keeps her out of sight in her condo unless he's alone. Then he hangs out at her place."

"So he's never by himself. Is there staff at his house?"

"Not full-time. He does have a part-time maid and butler, a couple that come in when he's entertaining. Husband and wife."

"But they don't live on the premises?"

"That's right."

"Do we know his schedule?"

"He's throwing a cocktail party this evening from five until seven. After that, he'll probably head for the condo."

"Does he drive or walk?"

"He's done both. Depends on how he's feeling, I suppose. There's no pattern."

"I'm guessing we can't get through the gate without being logged in or something, right?"

"Right. The guards have a list. If you're not on the list, they call the owner to get an okay."

"How big's the community? If we slipped in and walked around, would we be noticed?"

"Several villas are rentals, so strangers aren't too remarkable. We can probably get away with a little scouting. We'll just have to figure out how to get in. Shouldn't be too difficult; the security is mostly for show, I gather."

"You said it's gated; is it fenced?"

"There's decorative wrought iron fencing in the places that are visible. A lot of the perimeter is bounded by undeveloped property. There are a few strands of barbed wire through that. No barrier to two people on foot. We'll have to hike anywhere from a few hundred yards to half a mile to reach the fence line, though."

"Sounds like you've done your recon."

"Like I said, Lee was the next one on my list. I was sure he'd do something to blow his cover. So yeah, I scouted his place a few weeks ago."

"Then what's our agenda for the day? We've got several hours to kill."

"We need to go shopping. I don't have anything to wear."

I laughed.

"I'm serious. And you need clothes, too. We can't walk around an upscale golf resort looking like boat bums."

"Yes, ma'am. You have a place in mind?"

"South Beach. We'll park the car and play tourist at the Lincoln Road Mall. We should be able to find what we need there."

"Speaking of what we need, you mentioned drugs."

"All taken care of."

"Somebody's going to meet us?"

"Somebody already did."

"When?"

"At the car rental place. There's a stash in the well with the spare tire."

"How?"

"Friends. But we'll check, just to be sure."

"Okay. You're just full of surprises."

"I'm disappointed that you're surprised; it's what I do. You know that."

"I'm only surprised at the extent of your resources."

"The government's not the only high-stakes player in this game. Just because I'm self-employed doesn't mean I can't run with the big dogs. There's a reason my rates are high; I have lots of overhead."

"Frankie Dailey told me you were the best around, but I thought that was hyperbole."

"I don't know about the best. I only know I've built a solid business by paying attention to the small stuff. That's what trips up the amateurs."

"The devil's in the details," I said. "I almost feel like I'm along for the ride on this one."

"Not at all. Besides, I dragged you into this whole mess when I hitched a ride on *Island Girl*. So I owe you. Not to mention I've fallen for you, big time."

"Yeah. I know the feeling." *But I'm still wondering about how we got here. Way too many coincidences. And they just keep coming.*

"Think this'll do?" I asked, as I signaled a turn into a parking garage on 17th Street at Pennsylvania Avenue. That put us a short walk from Lincoln Road Mall.

"Looks good. I want to check that spare tire well, so see if you can find a spot where we won't attract too much attention when I rummage in the trunk."

Turning into the garage and following the ramp up a few levels until the parked cars were sparse, I pulled into a space in an unoccupied row. We got out, and I opened the trunk.

"I'll keep watch. Do what you need to," I said, as Mary began to move our luggage.

32

"You know," Mary said, "this is a pretty place, even though I can't fathom the attraction that golf holds for some people."

"It is. And I don't get golf, either."

We were sitting on a bench just off the 14th green, looking across the fairway at Senator Lee's house. The bench was on a slight rise in the ground, affording us a good view of the people socializing on Lee's pool deck.

They were about 75 yards away, so we couldn't identify them, but Lee himself was easy enough to pick out. The senator was moving from group to group, chatting, shaking hands, slapping backs, and moving on to someone else.

"Typical politician," Mary said. "Working the crowd. Wonder how punctual they'll be?"

I glanced at my watch. "It's 6:45. A bunch of people have already left. I'm betting this is all business. Nobody will stick around longer than they have to."

"Hope you're right," Mary said. "The mosquitos will find us soon."

The sun was low in the sky behind us; we were sitting in shadow, although the golden light from the beginning of a south Florida sunset bathed Lee's pool deck. The light was fading rapidly, and the crowd was thinning even more quickly. In the gathering dusk, flood lights came on, illuminating the pool deck. The last few people were saying their goodbyes.

"Like a signal, those lights," Mary said.

"Spoils the mood, for sure. They must be on some kind of sensor."

"Or maybe a timer." Mary looked at her watch. "It's seven o'clock, on the nose."

In another ten minutes, Lee was alone except for the man and woman who were picking up the dishes and glassware. Lee walked up to the man and spoke with him for a few seconds. The man nodded and waved the woman over. They talked with Lee for a few minutes and left, going toward a side yard that was mostly paved. There was a nondescript, older-model car parked there. The couple got in it and drove away.

"Game on," Mary said, as we watched Lee go indoors.

While we were walking across the fairway, the floodlights went dark.

"Hope he's not in too big a hurry to get to his honey," I said.

"We'll be okay." Mary took a phone from the pocket of her slacks and made a call. "Keep him on the phone for a couple of minutes," she said. "We're moving in, but we want him to stay inside." She put the phone away.

"Who did you call?"

"Part of the overhead I'm paying for. Someone who's been posing as an anonymous donor to Lee's campaign."

By now, we were working our way through the shrubbery that separated Lee's pool area from the fairway. A wall of French doors opened from a large indoor living area onto the pool deck. We could see Lee standing at a desk, his back to us, a phone pressed to the side of his head.

Ten feet from one of the open doors, Mary stopped in the shadow of a potted palm, her hand on my arm. We watched until he hung up the phone, and then Mary made her move, stepping through the doorway into the living room.

"Excuse me, Senator," she said, pausing inside the door.

Lee whirled to face her, then his face broke into a grin as he ran his eyes up and down her curves. "Yes? I don't... "

"Sorry to intrude, but I seem to have been abandoned. I guess I bored Gerry, or something."

"Gerry?" Lee frowned and shook his head. "I don't think I remember a Gerry, but he's a fool if he left you here with me. Have we met?"

Mary tossed her hair and shot her hip, tilting her head. "No, but I've dreamed of a chance to be alone with you. I think you're the hottest man in the Senate."

Lee smiled. "What's your name, beautiful?" He approached her, his movements as graceful as if he were dancing.

"Mary," she said.

"I'm Jeff, to my friends. Can I offer you a drink, Mary?"

"Later, maybe," she said, stepping in close to him and putting her arms around his neck, tilting her head back, lips parted.

He took the bait. She turned a little, leaning against the desk. Lee turned with her, lifting her so she was sitting on the edge of the desk as he pawed her. She unbuckled his belt and worked his pants down over his ample hips.

He was so excited he never even felt the hypodermic when I stuck it in his ass. His first clue that something was wrong came when she shoved him away and he fell into my arms.

He was woozy and unsteady on his feet as I half-led, half-dragged him to the couch nearby. Mary doused most of the lights and picked up a remote control with the label "Drapes" from his desk.

"Just in case somebody else is out there on the golf course," she said, as she closed the drapes. "Might as well have a little privacy."

"Yeah, baby. Privacy," Lee said, with a goofy grin on his face.

He was so out of it he didn't even seem to notice me. When I handed Mary a pair of surgical gloves, he was still conscious, grinning at her as she pulled them on and wiped the remote control.

"Did I touch anything else?" she asked.

"No."

"Good. Let's pull his pants back up. He's not quite ready yet, anyway."

"Pants," Lee said, as I lifted him so she could square away his clothes.

"There," she said. "All better, now."

"All better," Lee said.

"You comfortable, Senator?"

"Comfortable. I'm Jeff." His head rolled to the side.

"We're going to play a little game, Jeff," Mary said.

"Game..."

"That's right. It's like a guessing game. I'm going to ask you questions, and you're going to give me the answers. If you get the answers wrong, I win, and I get to do anything I want with you. If you win, you get to do whatever you want to me. Sound good?"

"Good." Lee snickered.

"I thought so. But just to make sure we both play fair, my friend Finn's going to keep score, and he'll tell me some of the questions. Okay?"

"Okay, Finn," Lee said, a vacant grin on his face as he looked up at me.

"So, Finn," Mary said. "Give me the first question."

33

IT WAS A LITTLE BEFORE 10 P.M. WHEN OUR RENTAL CAR PULLED up to the four-way stop. I was waiting in the undergrowth a few yards from the intersection. One of the roads bordered the south end of the gated community where Lee lived.

Covering our tracks after we finished with Lee, Mary and I split up when we left his villa. She went northwest across the golf course to retrieve the car, while I headed south to our prearranged rendezvous point at the four-way stop. As I got in the front passenger seat, she gave me a smile.

"Hey, sailor. Looking for a good time?"

"Nah," I said. "I'm taken. But a ride would be nice."

"What do you think?" she asked, pulling away from the stop. "Surprised by what we got from Lee?"

"Yes."

After we finished picking Lee's brain, we waited for the second, lethal dose of anesthetic to take effect. We didn't want to leave until we were sure he was dead. While Mary monitored his passing, I cleaned up the evidence of our presence and planted the suicide note she brought. This was our first chance to compare notes on what we learned from the senator.

"Me, too," she said. "I'm still trying to understand how they linked both of us to Kelley's death, and so quickly. That's a little alarming."

"It must have been supposition, based on what they got from Nora," I said. "Either that, or she just flat-out told Lee — or some go-between — that you and I were both there. Maybe they beat it out of her. She seemed to know you were in the neighborhood; remember, she asked if you were with me when I called her before I went to her room."

"I thought you said she asked if you were alone."

"You're right. She did. But that was because she knew we were both in the BVI."

Mary nodded. "That could be. Do you recognize the name Phyllis Greer?"

Lee told us that my boss, Phyllis Greer, was the source of their information about my daughter.

"No, but it has to be the name they had for Nora. She wasn't really named Nora Thomas; the way she told me that was her name when we met in St. Martin gave that away."

"Or it could be her boss, that undersecretary you mentioned. You never had a name for her, right?"

"Right. I don't even know if it's a her or a him. But somehow that doesn't seem likely."

"Why do you say that?"

"If Lee and company had the undersecretary on the string, why would they have needed to use Nora in St. Thomas? They could have just cut to the chase with my daughter."

Mary rubbed her chin, driving with one hand. "You may have something there. But if Nora, or whatever her name was — if she were working with them, gone rogue, as you put it — why would they have killed her?"

I pondered that for a moment. "Good question. But you were the one who first raised the possibility that she was on their payroll, remember?"

"Yes," Mary said. "I remember. When we were about to eat lunch in St. Thomas, after we killed Kelley and those guys. But we never followed through on that thought."

"No," I said. "We got wrapped up in your fantasy, instead."

"You said it was your fantasy, too, Finn."

"It was; it is. I wasn't blaming you. Just trying to retrace our steps."

I was looking at her as she concentrated on driving. She spared me a glance and said, "Then we got derailed by the text from the kidnappers. And here we are."

"Yes," I said. "Here we are. Nora could have gone rogue, or not. Hard to tell, now. What Kelley did to her was over the top, anyway. I still wonder about it. You're suggesting the undersecretary threw Nora under the bus?"

"I don't know, Finn. Maybe Nora was onto them. If the undersecretary suspended her because she asked about Kelley at your request, and then they tailed her to St. Martin... See what I mean?"

"Yes. You're making her out to be one of the good guys."

"Well, I'm just saying it's possible. Maybe they decided to let Kelley burn her to get your attention, like Kelley said."

I thought about that for a few seconds and shook my head. "What a mess. But with people like that, it's tough to understand their motives. Maybe Kelley had his own reasons for wanting Nora out of the picture."

"Nora's an enigma," Mary said.

"Maybe. After what Lee said, I think she was one of them. They probably had Kelley waste her to cover their tracks. Too many signs point to her being corrupt."

"There's no way I can see to resolve that now," Mary said. "Too late to ask the three of them any more questions. Think you can find out who the undersecretary is?"

"I can try, but that one's buried deep. We might have more luck with Lee's mystery man."

"It's not going to be easy to figure out who that is, either," Mary said.

When we pressed Lee on the subject of who was giving him his orders, he only said, "The man who took over from O'Hanlon."

No matter how we phrased the question, Lee couldn't identify the man.

Lee met him once, but Lee was blindfolded. Asked about the man's voice, Lee said he never heard it before. Two men picked him up and took him to meet his new contact after O'Hanlon's death. That's when he first heard the man speak. His voice was distinctive, easily recognized over the telephone. Lee described it as having just a hint of an accent, but not one he could place. Lee never saw the man or his two messengers again.

The new man established his credentials by rattling off all the things that O'Hanlon knew about Lee. That included some embarrassing facts about things Lee did aboard O'Hanlon's yacht years earlier.

"There must be a clue in those files of yours," I said.

"Maybe. Have you talked to your code-breaker friend? About the files?"

"Not yet, but that's the next thing on my list. Speaking of lists, let's talk about where we go from here."

"Okay. What are you thinking we should do next?"

"Given that they have us both linked to the Kelley hit, we might want to put some space between us for a while."

Mary let out a loud sigh and took her eyes off the road to look at me for a long moment.

"Relieved or disappointed?" I asked.

"Yes. Both. Disappointed because I know you're right. Relieved because now I don't have to persuade you. Teaming up on two hits in a row might be seen as a pattern."

"Only if somebody knows we were both on the Lee job," I

said. "I'm the one with the clear motive." *Let's see how you
respond to that one. Who knew you were going to kill Lee, besides
your pal Phorcys?*

"That's so. But Lee knew I was part of the Kelley job, and we
traveled from the VI to Miami together. Plus, they've got me
down as the one who wiped out the remains of O'Hanlon's
bunch. I've got the same worry you do. We need to split up for a
while."

"I'll miss you," I said.

"I know. I'll miss you, too. But it's only until we get this
sorted out."

I nodded. "Got any ideas on how to split up?"

"The car's in my name, and I know my way around Florida.
How about if I drop you off at the Miami airport? You can head
back to *Island Girl.*"

"Works for me. There're plenty of early morning flights
that'll put me in puddle-jumper range of Tortola. Drop me at
one of the airport hotels; I'll get a room and crash for a while.
What're you going to do?"

"Stay out of sight and see if I can figure out who's picking up
the pieces of O'Hanlon's empire. We can use the blind email
drop to compare notes, and maybe slip in some calls on burner
phones. Keep me up to date about breaking the code for the
names in the files. That could make a big difference to me."

"Yes, I will. I have a few ideas; I may give it a whirl on my
own. I've got idle time ahead of me, sounds like."

"You worried about using your code breaker friend?"

"Yes, until I figure out what's going on with Nora's replacement. That's assuming they even want to keep me on the team."

"You think they might not?"

"I don't know."

"If somebody stepped into her job, how would they go
about approaching you?"

"Cautiously. A real replacement would have all kinds of

background information they could use to convince me they were legit."

"Then you think there are people there besides Nora who would know about you?"

"Yes. After all, this is the government. I don't know if the undersecretary knows who I am. But you can bet they know how many people there are like me, and how Nora kept in touch with us. It won't be quick and clean. There'll be lots of dancing around on both sides while we check each other out. I went through that with Nora, years ago."

"Is the person she replaced still around?"

"Maybe. If he is, that could make it quicker, but I wouldn't count on it."

"Can I ask a super-personal question, Finn?"

"Sure. Ask."

"Do you even want to keep your relationship with them?"

"I've gone both ways on that since all this happened. On the one hand, it's all I know. On the other, there's this woman in my life now. Part of me wishes we could put all this excitement behind us and have a normal, boring life."

"Are you mocking me?"

"Mocking you? Why do you — "

"Because of my fantasy. I — "

"No, Mary. I'm not mocking you. When you told me about that, well, that's when I knew for sure that... Well, like I said when you told me, it's my fantasy too."

"Hold on to that, Finn. If we both want it to happen, we'll make it happen."

"I don't know if it'll be that easy. They may not let me go; a person like me, with all my secrets — I'm a hell of a liability."

"I understand. But what can they do if you don't want to play their game anymore?"

"You know damn well what they can do. I'm an expendable asset to them."

"Yes. I get that. But you told me once you were hard to kill."

"Hard. But not impossible."

"That was before you teamed up with me, partner. You may not be immortal now, but you're at least twice as hard to kill as you were before you had me watching your back. If you want out, I'll help."

"Sounds like a recruiting pitch." I winked at her. "What is it you want from me, and who would I be working for?"

"I want your undying love and affection. And you'd be working for us."

"Who's us?"

"You and me, you cynical old man. Us. Nobody else."

"Who do I have to kill to get the job?" I asked, grinning at her.

"I don't know yet, but I'll let you know. Keep checking the email drop."

She turned onto the airport access road and followed the signs for lodging. "I'll meet you in Puerto Real in about two weeks. Just give it enough time for the dust to clear, and then we can start over," she said.

Pulling into the parking area of a seedy looking motel with a neon "Vacancy" sign, she stopped the car. "You promised me uninhabited islands. I've been thinking about that. We could..."

She gave me one of those smiles as she let her unfinished sentence hang in the silence.

"What do you think?" she asked, finally.

"Not Puerto Real. We already did that; somebody might remember. Head for Guánica. I'll be anchored in Bahia Guánica. Know where it is?"

"South coast, right?"

"Yes. You been there?"

"Not yet, but I'm looking forward to it. And those islands."

She leaned across the console. Wrapping her arms around me, she gave me a soft, lingering kiss.

"Stay well, sailor. See you soon."

"Yes, ma'am. You take care."

As I got out, she popped the trunk. I retrieved my duffle bag and closed the lid. She blew me a kiss in the rear-view mirror and pulled out into traffic. I shouldered my duffle bag and went inside.

34

THERE WERE PLENTY OF SEATS ON THE EARLY BIRD FLIGHT TO ST. Thomas. I bought a ticket and cleared security as soon as they opened. Forty minutes before boarding, I stood at a plate-glass window looking out at the planes on the taxiway.

When I went through security, they made me turn on my laptop and the satellite phone. As I was putting the phone away, I saw there was a voicemail. That alarmed me. There was only one other phone that could call my sat phone. That was Nora's sat phone, and Nora was dead.

On my way to the gates, I kept an eye on the signal strength indicator on the sat phone. Service could be tricky indoors. The phone acquired a solid signal through the windows, and I was out of the traffic pattern between security and the gates, so I had a little privacy. I stopped and leaned back against the glass.

Taking a deep breath, I thought about what I was about to do before pressing the sat phone's green button. The time stamp on the screen for the voicemail notification was from 8:37 last night. That was when Mary and I were interrogating Lee. The phone was in my bag in the trunk of the rental car then, so it didn't have service. Besides, it wasn't turned on then. The last time I used it was before we met Nora and Kelley in St. Thomas, and I turned it off right after Nora told me where to meet her.

I powered it on and waited for it to boot up when I was at the security checkpoint a few minutes ago. The phone must have acquired a signal at the security checkpoint and down-loaded the voicemail notification then, while I was messing with my laptop.

Nora gave me this phone when I met her in St. Martin a few days ago. She confirmed then that no one else knew about it. Only she had the number, she assured me. Mary and I saw Nora die about 36 hours before the voicemail was left, so some-body besides Nora left it.

When she gave this phone to me, Nora also told me the phone's location tracking function was disabled, but now I wondered. After hearing from Senator Lee that Nora betrayed me, I couldn't trust anything she told me.

If she lied about the tracking function, somebody could have picked up my location when I turned the phone on at security. Retrieving the message wouldn't increase my exposure much at this point.

Whoever found the bodies of Nora and Kelley and the two goons must have taken Nora's phone and left the voicemail. Then it sunk in with me that nobody but Nora knew how to unlock *her* sat phone.

I decided to retrieve the voicemail and see who left it. Then I would sanitize the phone and dispose of it. I entered all the codes and called voicemail, nearly dropping the phone when I heard the message.

"Hi, Finn. Don't hang up; it's really me. I know this is a shock based on what you thought you saw at the resort yester-day, but trust me. I'm okay, and we need to talk. It's too compli-cated for voicemail, so call me when you get this. It's urgent that I let you know what's happening."

It was Nora's voice. I listened to the recorded date and time at the end of the message, just in case the time stamp on my phone's screen was wrong. It wasn't. Rattled, I thought about the possibilities. The message was from last night — 36 hours after Kelley's man blew Nora's head off.

There could have been somebody besides Kelley and his two thugs involved in interrogating Nora. Maybe she gave up the unlock codes for the phone. But I recognized her voice.

Could they have forced her to record the message in advance? Why would they have done that? Did they expect that they would need to track me down? If so, I just gave away my location. Might as well go for broke.

I entered the unlock code again and called Nora's phone.

"Hello, Finn," she answered. "Thanks for trusting me. Obviously, what happened at the resort the day before yesterday was staged. I'll tell you as much as I can, okay?"

"I saw that guy blow somebody's brains out through the side of that black cloth bag. That clearly wasn't you, but — "

"But you heard my voice. I was in an adjoining room with a transmitter. There was a receiver and a speaker in the bag over that woman's head. It was a setup."

"You set me up?"

"No, not you. We set up Kelley. We knew he was dirty."

"But you couldn't have been sure we'd kill him."

"You weren't supposed to kill him. You said you were alone. We were going to tape his demand for the girl and the files and use it to hang him."

This wasn't making sense. And who was "we?" "Why did Kelley trust you, if he was dirty?"

"We double-crossed him. We convinced him that we thought you were the dirty one, that you were working with that girl and the people trying to take over from O'Hanlon. We made him think we were setting *you* up. But *he* was really our target."

"What about the woman?"

"Like I said, we weren't expecting the girl to be with you. You told me you were alone, remember? We thought she was in—"

"Not her," I said. "The woman Kelley's guy shot — the one I thought was you. That wasn't staged."

"Yes, it was."

"They killed her, Nora. I know what a head shot at close range looks like. That was the real thing."

"Oh, yeah. Sure. But she was expendable. That was part of the setup; she had it coming. She was going to die anyway."

"And what made you think I wouldn't kill Kelley and his boys?"

"You said you were alone. We didn't expect the girl to come in."

"You know my skills. *The girl*, as you call her, was incidental. I was about to take out Kelley and his two goons when she came in. I knew she might show up, but I wasn't counting on it. Those guys were complete amateurs; they couldn't get out of their own way. You know my track record; they were dead when they let me walk in that room without killing me on the spot."

"It's a relief to hear you haven't lost your confidence."

"Uh-huh. So let's see if I understand what you're telling me. You thought I would walk in and watch Kelley kill the woman who was posing as you. After he showed me how serious he was, I would agree to turn over *the girl* and the files within 48 hours and, then I would walk out of the room. Was that the plan?"

"In essence, yes. I planned to catch up with you right after you left. We would have busted Kelley, and I would have filled you in."

"And then what?"

"We planned to flip Kelley and go after the people up the line from him."

"I see. So this was all a setup to make Kelley roll over?"
"Yes."
"And who is this 'we' you keep referring to?"
"You know I can't tell you that."
"What about your suspension from duty?"
"Part of the setup."
"Why not trust me to be part of the team?"
"Need to know."
Somehow, I knew we would get to that point.
"Where do we go from here?" I asked.
"Your mission is complete. Enjoy your retirement for a while. Just kick back and take it easy. I'll be in touch one of these days, when I have another project for you. Meanwhile, you've earned a nice bonus for this job. Any more questions?"
Like you would answer them. "Um, yes. About this phone..."
"Hang on to it. That one's not compromised."
"You told me location tracking wasn't enabled."
"Oh, right. I forgot about that. Don't worry; I can have that fixed remotely. Give me 24 hours and I'll be able to find you again, just like old times. And I like your new girlfriend."
"Glad you approve. I've got to move. I'm starting to attract attention. Thanks for the recap. Later."
With that, I disconnected the call and snapped the battery pack off the back of the phone. Using my fingernail, I opened the SIM carrier and removed the SIM. I walked up the concourse toward the gate for my flight, stopping in the men's room.
In one of the stalls, I wrapped the SIM in toilet tissue and flushed it. I went out to the sinks and pretended to wash my hands while I made sure I was alone. Satisfied, I wiped the phone to get rid of my prints and dropped it in the large waste-basket with the wet paper towels. Picking up the wastebasket, I shook it vigorously to settle the phone close to the bottom.
I used another damp paper towel to scrub my prints from

the battery pack and wrapped it in the used towel. On my way to the gate, I dropped the battery pack in another waste bin next to a fast-food place.

At the gate, I checked in and sat down with my duffle bag between my feet. They wouldn't board my flight for a few minutes; I would use the time to consider my next move.

Nora or Phyllis? Whatever her name was, I wasn't finished with her. She may have been lying about location tracking being disabled in the phone. She lied about enough other things. If the tracking function was on, she could put me in the neighborhood of Lee's villa around the time he overdosed. She could also track me to the Miami airport, but after that, she would have a harder time.

She was telling part of the truth about the encounter at the resort in St. Thomas. It was a setup, all right, but Kelley wasn't the target. Mary was. And my daughter. I would never forgive Nora for that. Nora was crooked, as Mary suggested earlier. And I wasn't through avenging my daughter's kidnapping. Not by a long way. We made Lee pay, and Mary's friend Phorcys took care of the people who snatched Abby, but Nora was still out there. For a while, anyway.

Nora was working with whoever was paying Kelley, and they wanted the files Mary took. That was consistent with the senator's story about Phyllis Greer, as he referred to Nora.

And she made no reference on the phone just now to my daughter's kidnapping. Why didn't she try to explain that away? Was it possible she didn't know about it? But Kelley knew; he mentioned "leverage you can't even imagine" when his thug killed that woman.

It made no sense that Nora failed to mention Abby's kidnapping. Unless she was feigning ignorance to keep up the pretense that she was setting up Kelley.

If that story were true, it would have been possible she didn't know about the kidnapping. That was a nice try, clever on Nora's part. But that story wasn't true. It overlooked the other evidence of her guilt.

Nora didn't know Senator Lee was dead, or she would have guessed her charade was over. When she got the news, she wouldn't believe he committed suicide. She knew too much about this business.

It was still too early for the senator's body to have been discovered. When Mary and I questioned him a few hours ago, he told us his mistress was waiting for him in the Bahamas. He planned to meet her there this evening.

With the mistress away, his maid and butler would be the most likely ones to find him. They were scheduled to go to his place later this afternoon to finish cleaning up after last night's party. I saw the notation on his desk calendar when I planted the suicide note on his desk. His body wouldn't be discovered for a while yet. So Nora didn't know.

When she found out Lee was dead, Nora would conclude that Mary or I killed him. Further, she would assume that we interrogated him and learned about her duplicity.

If she already suspected that, she would have made an effort to distance herself from Abby's kidnapping in our conversation a few minutes ago. But she didn't, so she was trying to hide her deceitfulness, damn her.

As soon as Lee's body was found, Nora would order my death. By then, I would be well-hidden.

But she would find me eventually. In fact, I would help her; I wanted to be found — at a time of my choosing.

Nora told me she would be in touch when she was ready to give me a new target. But my sights were already on my next target.

Satisfied with my analysis, I dug the laptop out of my duffle bag and logged onto the airport's WiFi network. Using my VPN and encryption software, I navigated to the blind email drop Mary and I were using and left her a message.

Emergency change of plans. We have an urgent joint mission, Partner. Get to Bahia Guánica ASAP. Forget the two-week timetable. I'll be there in three days; I'm making a detour to gather supplies. Whatever you were going to do to kill time for the next two weeks, skip it. This is more critical.

The risk to us will escalate fast once they discover that guy killed himself, so the two-week break we planned is riskier than moving ahead now. No need to pretend we weren't working together on those two jobs; they know already.

Our number one suspect lives to fight again, but she doesn't know we've found her out. No longer any question about her status; she's a target. She knows too much to let her stay alive. She's a traitor to all I've sworn to uphold. Besides, she was part of this whole O'Hanlon mess.

Hurry home. Those uninhabited islands beckon.

Love, Finn

I missed her already, but it wouldn't be for long. By the time I sailed *Island Girl* to Bahia Guánica, Mary would be on her way there. Then we could plan the opening moves in our next game. Nora wouldn't be an easy target, but she was no match for Mary and me. I felt a smile coming as I drifted off to sleep, to dream of my *real* island girl.

THE END

MAILING LIST

Thank you for reading *Avengers and Rogues*.

Sign up for my mailing list at http://eepurl.com/bKujyv for notice of new releases and special sales or giveaways. I'll email a link to you for a free download of my short story, The Lost Tourist Franchise, when you sign up. I promise not to use the list for anything else; I dislike spam as much as you do.

A NOTE TO THE READER

Thank you again for reading *Avengers and Rogues*, the second book in the **J.R. Finn Sailing Mystery Series**. I hope you enjoyed it. If so, please leave a brief review on Amazon.

Reviews are of great benefit to independent authors like me; they help me more than you can imagine. They are a primary means to help new readers find my work. A few words from you can help others find the pleasure that I hope you found in this book, as well as keeping my spirits up as I work on the next one.

In September 2020, I published *Sharks and Prey*, the eighth novel in the **J.R. Finn Sailing Mystery** series. This series is also available in audiobook format.

———

I also write two other sailing-thriller series set in the Caribbean. If you enjoyed the adventures of Finn and Mary, you'll enjoy the **Bluewater Thrillers** and the **Connie Barrera Thrillers**.

The **Bluewater Thrillers** feature two young women, Dani

Berger and Liz Chirac. Dani and Liz sail a luxury charter yacht named *Vengeance*. They often find trouble, but they can take care of themselves.

The **Connie Barrera Thrillers** are a spin-off from the **Bluewater Thrillers**. Before Connie went to sea, she was a first-rate con artist. Dani and Liz met Connie in *Bluewater Ice*, and they taught her to sail. She liked it so much she bought a charter yacht of her own.

Dani and Liz also introduced her to Paul Russo, a retired Miami homicide detective. Paul signed on as her first mate and chef, but he ended up as her husband. Connie and Paul run a charter sailing yacht named *Diamantista*. Like Dani and Liz, they're often beset by problems unrelated to sailing.

The **Bluewater Thrillers** and the **Connie Barrera Thrillers** share many of the same characters. Phillip Davis and his wife Sandrine, Sharktooth, and Marie LaCroix often appear in both series, as do Connie, Paul, Dani, and Liz. Here's a link to the web page that lists those novels in order of publication: http://www.clrdougherty.com/p/bluewater-thrillers-and-connie-barrera.html

———

If you'd like to know when my next book is released, visit my author's page on Amazon at www.amazon.com/author/clrdougherty and click the "Follow" link or sign up for my mailing list at http://eepurl.com/bKujyv for information on sales and special promotions. I welcome email correspondence about books, boats and sailing. My address is clrd@clrdougherty.com. I enjoy hearing from people who read my books; I always answer email from readers. Thanks again for your support.

ABOUT THE AUTHOR

Welcome aboard!

Charles Dougherty is a lifelong sailor; he's lived what he writes. He and his wife have spent over 30 years sailing together.

For 15 years, they lived aboard their boat full-time, cruising the East Coast and the Caribbean islands. They spent most of that time exploring the Eastern Caribbean.

Dougherty is well acquainted with the islands and their people. The characters and locations in his novels reflect his experience.

A storyteller before all else, Dougherty lets his characters speak for themselves. Pick up one of his thrillers and listen to the sound of adventure as you smell the salt air. Enjoy the views of distant horizons and meet some people you won't forget.

Dougherty's sailing fiction books include the **Bluewater Thrillers**, the **Connie Barrera Thrillers**, and the **J.R. Finn Sailing Mysteries**.

Dougherty's first novel was *Deception in Savannah*. While it's not about sailing, one of the main characters is Connie Barrera. He had so much fun with Connie that he built a sailing series around her.

Before writing Connie's series, he wrote the first three Bluewater Thrillers, about two young women running a charter yacht in the islands. In the fourth book, Connie shows up as their charter guest.

She stayed for the fifth Bluewater book. Then Connie demanded her own series.

The J.R. Finn books are his newest sailing series. The first Finn book, though it begins in Puerto Rico, starts with a real-life encounter that Dougherty had in St. Lucia. For more information about that, visit his website.

Dougherty's other fiction works are the *Redemption of Becky Jones*, a psycho-thriller, and *The Lost Tourist Franchise*, a short story about another of the characters from Deception in Savannah.

Dougherty has also written two non-fiction books. *Life's a Ditch* is the story of how he and his wife moved aboard their sailboat, Play Actor, and their adventures along the east coast of the U.S. *Dungda de Islan'* relates their experiences while cruising the Caribbean.

Charles Dougherty welcomes email correspondence with readers.

www.clrdougherty.com
clrd@clrdougherty.com

OTHER BOOKS BY C.L.R. DOUGHERTY

Bluewater Thrillers

Bluewater Killer

Bluewater Vengeance

Bluewater Voodoo

Bluewater Ice

Bluewater Betrayal

Bluewater Stalker

Bluewater Bullion

Bluewater Rendezvous

Bluewater Ganja

Bluewater Jailbird

Bluewater Drone

Bluewater Revolution

Bluewater Enigma

Bluewater Quest

Bluewater Target

Bluewater Blackmail

Bluewater Clickbait

Bluewater Thrillers Boxed Set: Books 1-3

Connie Barrera Thrillers

From Deception to Betrayal - An Introduction to Connie Barrera

Love for Sail - A Connie Barrera Thriller

Sailor's Delight - A Connie Barrera Thriller

A Blast to Sail - A Connie Barrera Thriller

Storm Sail - A Connie Barrera Thriller

Running Under Sail - A Connie Barrera Thriller

Sails Job - A Connie Barrera Thriller

Under Full Sail - A Connie Barrera Thriller

An Easy Sail - A Connie Barrera Thriller

A Torn Sail - A Connie Barrera Thriller

A Righteous Sail - A Connie Barrera Thriller

Sailor Take Warning - A Connie Barrera Thriller

Sailor's Choice - A Connie Barrera Thriller

J.R. Finn Sailing Mysteries

Assassins and Liars

Avengers and Rogues

Vigilantes and Lovers

Sailors and Sirens

Villains and Vixens

Killers and Keepers

Devils and Divas

Sharks and Prey

Other Fiction

Deception in Savannah

The Redemption of Becky Jones

The Lost Tourist Franchise

Books for Sailors and Dreamers

Life's a Ditch

Dungda de Islan'

Audiobooks

Assassins and Liars

Avengers and Rogues

Vigilantes and Lovers

Sailors and Sirens

Villains and Vixens

Killers and Keepers

Devils and Divas

Sharks and Prey

For more information please visit www.clrdougherty.com

Or visit www.amazon.com/author/clrdougherty

Made in the USA
Las Vegas, NV
01 March 2022

44741945R00115